Magical Tales
FROM
Many Lands

ALSO ILLUSTRATED

BY *Jane Ray*

The Story of the Creation

La Historia de la Creación

The Story of Christmas

La Historia de Navidad

Noah's Ark

MAGICAL TALES
from
MANY LANDS

RETOLD BY MARGARET MAYO

ILLUSTRATED BY *Jane Ray*

DUTTON CHILDREN'S BOOKS ◆ NEW YORK

To Peter M.M.

To Ben Horsburgh J.R.

Library of Congress Cataloging-in-Publication Data

Mayo, Margaret.
Magical Tales from Many Lands / retold by Margaret Mayo;
illustrated by Jane Ray.—1ˢᵗ American ed.   p.   cm.
Summary: Presents an international collection of
tales, including "The Lemon Princess,"
"Seven Clever Brothers," and "Baba Yaga Bony-Legs."
ISBN 0-525-45017-3
1. Fairy tales [1. Fairy tales. 2. Folklore.] I. Ray, Jane, ill. II. Title.
PZ8.M4572Mag 1993 [398.2]—dc21 93-12164 CIP AC

First published in the United States 1993
by Dutton Children's Books,
a division of Penguin Putnam Books for Young Readers
345 Hudson Street, New York, New York 10014
Originally published in Great Britain 1993
by Orchard Books, London
Typography by Adrian Leichter
Printed in Malaysia
First American Edition

3   5   7   9   10   8   6   4   2

CONTENTS

✦ *The Lemon Princess* ✦

Once, in those faraway times when toads had wings and camels could fly, a king and queen had an only son, called Prince Omar. The day came when they decided he must do what every other prince does—he must find a beautiful girl and marry her. So Prince Omar looked for a beautiful wife, *but*—and it was a big *but*—he could not find a girl who was beautiful enough.

One day an old woman came to him. "My lord prince," she said, "let me tell you about a princess—an exceedingly beautiful princess—whose face has not yet been touched by the sun. She is the one you seek. She is your fate."

"And how can I find this beautiful princess?" he asked.

"You must ride eastward for three days and three nights," said the old woman. "Then you will come to a garden surrounded by roses, with a lemon tree in it that bears only three ripe lemons. Pick the lemons, but be very careful not to cut them open until you come to a place with plenty of water."

The next morning Prince Omar mounted his horse and set off. He rode eastward for three days and three nights, until he came to a garden with a hedge of roses growing around it. He opened the gate and walked in, and it was not long before he found the lemon tree with its three ripe lemons. So the prince picked them and rode back the way he had come.

Now, he had not gone far before he began to wonder what was inside those lemons. He chose one, took a knife, and cut it open. Then there rose up from the lemon an exceedingly beautiful girl. "Water!" she called out. "Please give me water!"

But there was no water anywhere around. The next moment, the girl simply faded away and was gone.

Prince Omar was sad. But the thing was done, and there was no going back. So he continued on his way.

It was not long, however, before he began to wonder about the other lemons and whether there were girls in them also. So he chose another one and cut it open with his knife. And there rose up from that lemon a girl who was even more beautiful than the first, and she too called out, "Water! Please give me water!"

But again there was no water anywhere around, and this girl also faded away and was gone.

"I see now that I must take great care of my third lemon," said the prince; and with that, he went on his way.

After a while he came to a river, and, remembering the old woman's advice, he took the third lemon and cut it open. And there rose up a girl who was even more beautiful than the two who had come before. Her eyes were as gentle as the moon, her skin as pale as ivory, her long black hair as soft as silk. She too called out, "Water! Please give me water!"

Well, Prince Omar was so anxious not to lose this beautiful girl that he took hold of her and dropped her in the river. Just like that. She drank the clear, fresh water until she was satisfied, and then she climbed out, naked though she was.

The prince took off his cloak and wrapped it around her. "My beautiful Lemon Princess," he said, "you, and you alone, shall be my bride. But before I take you to the palace, I must go and bring you fine clothes to wear and a horse to ride."

"Then I shall hide in this tall poplar tree until you return," said the Lemon Princess. And with that, she called out, "Bend down, tall tree! Bend down!"

Immediately the tree bent down. The Lemon Princess seated herself on the topmost branch, and the tree stood tall again. Then the prince rode off.

Time came and time went, and the Lemon Princess sat high in the tree and waited. Before too long, a servant girl—an ugly girl, with mean eyes, tangled hair, rough skin, and cracked lips—came to fill a water jar at the river. As she bent down, she saw the face of the beautiful Lemon Princess reflected in the clear water.

"There—see how beautiful I am!" the servant girl cried. "I always knew I was far too beautiful to be a servant!"

Then she heard someone laugh, and a voice called out, "Look up, not down!"

The servant girl looked up, and when she saw the Lemon Princess sitting at the very top of the poplar tree, she said, "What are you doing up there in that tall tree?"

The Lemon Princess answered, "I am waiting for my bridegroom, the royal prince, to return with fine clothes for me to wear and a fine horse for me to ride."

Then the servant girl thought some wicked, evil thoughts. "Oh, lady, lovely lady," she said, "let me come up and talk to you and help pass the weary hours while you wait."

Now, the Lemon Princess had grown a bit lonely, so she said, "Bend down, tall tree! Bend down!" The tree bent down, and the servant girl was soon up among the topmost branches.

"Oh, lady, lovely lady," said the servant girl, "who are you with your magic powers? Are you human? Or are you a houri?"

The Lemon Princess answered, "I am a houri, and now I have chosen to enter the world of humans and to become the Lemon Princess."

The servant girl said, "Oh, lady, lovely lady, let me comb your long black hair." And she began to comb the Lemon Princess's hair, and as she did, she found a hairpin stuck deep in the princess's shining locks.

"Oh, lady, lovely lady, what is this?" she asked.

"It is my talisman," said the Lemon Princess. "Do not touch it."

Immediately the servant girl pulled out the hairpin, and *whir-r-r!* the Lemon Princess changed into a white dove, which flew away in a flutter of wings.

The servant girl took off her own clothes and threw them into the river below, where they floated away. Then she wrapped the prince's cloak around herself and waited.

Now, when Prince Omar returned and saw the ugly servant girl in the poplar tree, he was amazed.

"What has happened?" he cried. "You have changed. Your skin is creased and rough."

"It was the sun, my lord," she said. "The scorching sun burned it."

"But your lips? Your lips that were soft as flowers. What about them?"

"It was the wind, my lord," she said. "The hot, dry wind cracked them."

"But your eyes that were so large and gentle?"

"It was the tears, my lord," she said. "The tears I wept when I thought you would never return have made them red and swollen."

"But your hair that was soft as silk?"

"It was the black crow, my lord," she said. "The black crow tried to build a nest in my hair and tangled it and made it rough."

Then the ugly servant girl climbed down from the tree. "Time is a great healer, my lord. Soon I shall be as I was before," she assured him.

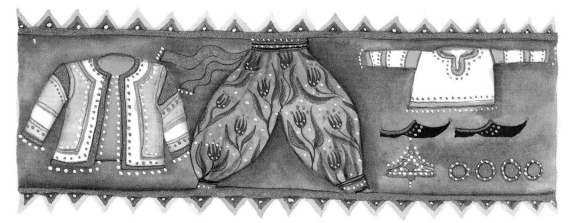

Prince Omar believed her, so he gave her beautiful clothes to wear—baggy trousers, blue as the summer sky; a white silk blouse embroidered with pearls; a jacket of gold thread; gold slippers; a gold headdress; and gold bracelets. Together they rode off to the palace.

Well, when the prince took the servant girl to the king and queen, they saw at once how ugly she was. "*This* is your chosen bride! Surely not!" was what they said.

"I have given her my word," the prince replied. "And in forty days our marriage will be celebrated."

Now, there was a garden around the king's palace. And before long a white dove began coming every morning to sit upon a sandalwood tree and sing. And every day Prince Omar came and stood beneath the tree and listened, and every day he said, "How sad is the song that the white dove sings!"

As soon as the servant girl noticed this, she went to the gardener. "The prince commands you to catch the white dove that sings the sad song in the sandalwood tree," she said. "You are to kill it and bury it deep in the ground."

The gardener did as he was told. He killed the bird and buried it.

But the next day, at the very place where the dove was buried, there stood a great cypress tree. And the wind came and sighed in its branches.

When the prince saw the tree, he was astonished. "What wonder is this!" he said. "A giant cypress where no tree stood before." When he heard the wind sighing, he said, "How sad is the sound of the wind in its branches!"

When the servant girl observed this, she went again to the gardener. "The prince commands you to cut down the cypress tree and make from its wood a cradle for the son I shall give him. Take any wood that remains and burn it."

The gardener did as he was told. He cut down the tree, and carpenters cut the wood into planks and made a cradle. Then the gardener gathered all the bits of wood that remained and built a fire. He was just going to throw the last small branch onto the flames when the prince's old nurse came by and asked the gardener for some firewood. And he gave her the small branch from the cypress tree.

The old nurse took the branch, put it down beside her fireplace, and then went off to market. But the moment she shut the door, the branch shivered and trembled all over, and soon it had changed into a girl. She was an exceedingly beautiful girl—the Lemon Princess herself.

Straightaway the princess set to work. She swept the floor. She washed the dishes. She peeled vegetables and prepared a meal. Then she hid behind a door.

When the old nurse returned home, she was very surprised. "Who has done all this?" she said. "A human or a spirit?"

The Lemon Princess came out from her hiding place, and she said, "I cleaned for you and I cooked for you, and now, please, will you do something for me? Go to Prince Omar and tell him that there lives in your house a girl who can make fine carpets, and if he will give you silk threads, she will make him the finest carpet ever seen."

So the old nurse went and spoke to the prince, and he ordered that she should be given silk threads and anything else that was needed. The Lemon Princess took needle and thread and set to work.

Time came and time went. At last the day arrived when Prince Omar was to marry the wicked servant girl. She had not changed; she was as ugly as ever. But the prince said to himself, "I have given my word and so I must marry her. Truly she must be the Lemon Princess! Who else could she be?"

But early on the morning of the wedding day, the old nurse took the beautiful finished carpet and went to the prince and said, "My lord prince, here is a wedding gift!"

Prince Omar unrolled the carpet, and he looked—and looked again. The princess had woven a picture of a garden surrounded by roses; in the center of the garden was the figure of the Lemon Princess herself.

"Who made this carpet?" the prince quickly asked.

"A girl who lives with me," answered the old nurse.

"Bring her to me at once," commanded the prince.

So the Lemon Princess came to the palace; and the moment Prince Omar saw her, he knew her.

"Truly," he said, "you alone are my beautiful Lemon Princess—my fate—the one who must be my bride. But tell me, where have you been? What happened to you these long and weary days?"

Then the Lemon Princess told Prince Omar about the wicked servant girl and her evil deeds. The prince was angry and sent his guards to find the servant girl. But as soon as she heard that she had been discovered, she ran right off. And she kept on running, at least until she crossed into the next kingdom. Some say she's running still!

Then, at last, there was a wedding, and Prince Omar married the beautiful Lemon Princess. The celebrations lasted for seven days and seven nights, and there was feasting, dancing, and great merriment for all.

Arabic

✦ Feather Woman ✦
and the Morning Star

One night in the moon of flowers, the time when the wild rose blooms and the grass is full upon the plains, a girl called Feather Woman took her blanket and slept outside her tepee with her younger sister. Just before dawn, Feather Woman woke and saw the morning star rising in the east. The star was so glorious that she could not take her eyes off it.

"Wake up and look over there at the morning star!" Feather Woman called to her sister "How I do love that star. It is the brightest and most beautiful of all!"

Her sister laughed and, teasing her, said, "So—you would like to marry a star!"

"It is true," Feather Woman answered quietly. "I would marry the morning star."

A few days later, Feather Woman was on her way to the river for water when she met a stranger on the trail. He was tall and erect and more handsome than any man she had ever seen. His clothes were of soft tanned skins that smelled of pine and sweet grass. He had a yellow feather in his hair, and in his hand he carried a juniper branch with a spider's web hanging from it.

"I am Morning Star," he said. "One night I saw you lying in the long grass and heard your words of love. Now I invite you to come to the Above World and live there with me."

Feather Woman trembled as she listened to his words. "First let me go to my mother and father and say good-bye," she said. "Then I will come with you."

But Morning Star answered, "You must come with me now or not at all."

He took the yellow feather and fastened it in her hair. Then he offered her the juniper branch and said, "Take this and close your eyes. The spider ladder will carry you to my home."

So Feather Woman took the juniper branch in her hand and closed her eyes. When she opened them again, she was in the sky, standing before a great tepee.

"Welcome to my home," said Morning Star. "This is the tepee of my father, the Sun, and of my mother, the Moon."

Now, at that time the Sun was away on his travels, but the kindly Moon was there. She welcomed her son's new bride and offered her food and drink. Then she gave her a soft tanned buckskin dress, a brace-

let of elk teeth, and an elkskin robe decorated with secret paintings.

The days passed, and Feather Woman was happy in the Above World. The Moon showed her all the flowers and vegetables and berries that grew there in abundance and taught her about herbs and secret medicines. She also gave her a digging stick made of wood that had been hardened in fire and showed her how to use the stick to dig up the many wild roots that were good to eat.

But the Moon warned Feather Woman that there was one plant that she must never dig up. This was the Giant Turnip, which grew near the tepee of the Spider Man, who wove the ladders by which the star people traveled between earth and sky. Many times the Moon told Feather Woman: "The Giant Turnip is sacred. If you touch it, you will bring unhappiness to us all."

Time passed. Morning Star and Feather Woman had a baby son, whom they called Star Boy. It seemed then that their happiness was complete.

But one day when Feather Woman was out collecting wild vegetables with her digging stick, she happened to pass the Giant Turnip. She said to herself, "I wonder what lies beneath the Giant Turnip."

Feather Woman walked all around it, then bent down and examined it more closely. She laid the baby on the ground and began to dig. She dug and she dug, but the turnip would not move. She dug some more, and finally the digging stick stuck fast underneath the turnip. Feather Woman looked up and saw two cranes flying overhead.

She called to them, "Come, mighty cranes! Come and help me move the Giant Turnip!"

The cranes circled above her three times and then landed. They took hold of the turnip top with their sharp beaks and rocked it to and fro. They sang a magic song and rocked it again until *prrr . . . mm!* It rolled out of the ground, leaving a giant hole where it had been growing.

Feather Woman knelt down and looked into the hole. To her surprise, she saw the camp of the Blackfeet Indians, where once she had lived. Smoke was rising from her parents' tepee. Children were laughing. Young men were playing games. The women were working—tanning hides, building tepees, gathering berries on the hillsides, and carrying water from the river.

Watching all this, Feather Woman longed to be back again upon the high plains with her own people. Slowly she got to her feet. She picked up Star Boy and held him close. When she turned to go home, there were tears in her eyes.

As soon as Morning Star saw his wife, he knew what she had done. "You have dug up the Giant Turnip!" he said.

That was all. Nothing more.

When the Moon heard what had happened, she was sad. But the Sun was very angry.

He said, "Feather Woman has disobeyed our command, and now she must return to earth. She has gazed again upon her own people and can no longer be happy here with us."

So Morning Star took his wife and his baby son to the tepee of the Spider Man and asked him to weave a ladder that would let them travel down to earth. Then he placed a digging stick in Feather Woman's hands, and he wrapped her and Star Boy in an elkskin robe.

"Close your eyes," he said. "And now, farewell."

When Feather Woman and her son arrived back on earth, it was an evening in the time when the berries are ripe. The Blackfeet Indians on the high plains looked up and saw a bright falling star. They ran to the place where it landed and found a strange bundle. When they opened it, there was Feather Woman with her baby. They recognized her as the girl who, many moons ago, had gone to collect water but had not returned.

From that time on, Feather Woman lived once again in her parents' tepee. And she shared with the Blackfeet Indians all the knowledge she had brought from the Above World. She taught them the secrets of the medicine plants. She showed them how to make and use a digging stick and how to recognize the wild potato, the wild turnip, the wild onion, and other plants good to eat.

But Feather Woman never forgot the Above World. On clear days, when the Sun shone, she would climb to the top of a high ridge and look up into the sky and think of her husband, the great and glorious Morning Star.

North American Indian

✦ The Kingdom Under the Sea ✦

One summer evening long ago, a lad called Urashima Taro was walking across the beach after a day's fishing when he saw a turtle lying helpless on its back, slowly waving its flippers. So he bent down and picked it up.

"You poor creature," he said. "I wonder who turned you upside down and left you here to die in the sun? Someone thoughtless, who knew no better, I suppose."

Urashima carried the turtle over the sands and waded into the sea as far out as he could. And as he let it go, he called, "Off you go, venerable turtle—and may you live for a thousand years!"

The next morning Urashima rowed out in his boat as usual, throwing his fishing line as he went. When he had passed the other boats and was

a long way out and all alone, he stopped rowing and let the boat drift on the waves.

It was then that he heard someone softly calling: "Urashima! Urashima Taro!"

He looked around, but there was no other boat in sight. Then he heard again: "Urashima! Urashima Taro!" It seemed to come from close by. So he looked again and saw a turtle swimming beside the boat.

"Turtle," he said, "was it you who called my name just now?"

"Yes, honorable fisherman, I was the one who spoke," answered the turtle. "Yesterday you saved my life, and today I have come to thank you and offer to take you to Ryn Jin, the palace of the Dragon King Under the Sea, who is my father."

Urashima was astonished. "The Dragon King Under the Sea is your father!" he said. "Surely not!"

"It is true. I am his daughter," the turtle answered. "And if you climb on my back, I will take you to him."

Urashima thought that it would be a fine thing to see the Kingdom Under the Sea, so he climbed out of the boat and sat himself down on the turtle's back.

Immediately they were off, skimming across the waves. And when it seemed they could go no faster, the turtle dived into the depths of the sea. Down they sped, passing whales and sharks, playful dolphins, and shoals of silvery fish. At last Urashima saw in the distance a magnificent coral gate decorated with pearls and glittering gems, and beyond it the long sloping roofs and gables of a coral palace.

"We are approaching the gateway of my father's palace," said the turtle, and even as she spoke, they reached it. "Now, from here, please, you must walk."

She turned to the swordfish who was the keeper of the gate and said, "This is an honored guest from the land of Japan. Please show him the way to go." And with that, she swam off.

The swordfish led Urashima into an outer courtyard, where a great

company of fish, row upon row of octopus and cuttlefish, bonito and plaice, bowed graciously toward him.

"Welcome to Ryn Jin, the palace of the Dragon King Under the Sea!" they chorused. "Welcome and thrice welcome!"

Then the great company of fish escorted Urashima to an inner court-yard, which led to the great door of the coral palace. When the door opened, there stood a radiantly beautiful princess. She wore flowing garments of red and green, shot through with all the colors of a wave in sunlight, and her long black hair streamed over her shoulders in the style of long ago.

"I welcome you to my father's kingdom," she said, "and ask you to stay here for a while in the land of everlasting youth, where summer never dies and sorrow never comes."

As Urashima listened to her words and gazed at her beautiful face, a feeling of contentment flooded over him. "My only wish is that I might stay here with you in this land forever," he said.

"Then I shall be your bride and we shall live together always," said the princess. "But first we must ask my father for his permission."

The princess took Urashima by the hand and led him through long corridors to her father's great hall. There they knelt before the mighty lord, the Dragon King Under the Sea, bowing so low that their foreheads touched the floor.

"Honorable father," said the princess, "this is the youth who saved my life in the land of men. If it pleases you, he is the one I have chosen to be my husband."

"It pleases me," the Dragon King answered, "but what does the fisher-lad say?"

"Oh . . . I gladly accept," said Urashima. It was all he could manage to say, so overwhelmed was he.

A wedding feast was arranged. And when the princess and Urashima had pledged their love, three times three, with a wedding cup of sake wine, the entertainments began. Soft music was played, and strange and wonderful rainbow-colored fish danced and sang.

The next day, when the celebrations were over, the princess showed

Urashima some of the marvels of her father's coral palace and his kingdom. The greatest of these by far was the garden of the four seasons.

To the east lay the garden of spring, where plum and cherry trees were in full blossom, and birds of all kinds sang sweetly. To the south the trees were clothed in the green of summer, and the crickets chirruped lazily. In the west chrysanthemums bloomed and the autumn maples were ablaze with flame-colored leaves. North stood the winter garden, where the bamboo trees and the earth lay covered in snow, and the ponds were thick with ice.

Now, there were so many things to see and wonder at in the Kingdom Under the Sea that Urashima forgot about his own home and his old life. But after a few days, he remembered his parents.

He said to the princess, "By now my mother and father must think that I have been drowned at sea. It must be three days or more since I left them. I must go immediately and tell them what has happened."

"Wait," urged the princess. "Wait a little longer. Stay here with me at least one more day."

"It is my duty to go and see my parents," he answered. "But I will return to you."

"Then I must become a turtle again and carry you to the land above the waves," she said. "But before you leave, accept this gift from me."

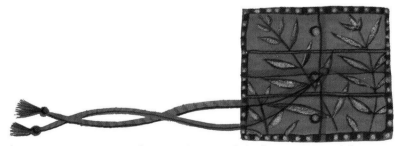

And the princess gave him a beautiful three-tiered lacquered box, tied around with a red silk cord.

"Keep this box with you always, but do not open it, whatever happens," she told him.

Urashima promised that he would do as she said and not open the box.

Once again the princess became a turtle, Urashima sat astride her back, and they were off. For a long time they rode through the sea, and when it seemed as if they had been traveling for days, they soared upward and reached the surface. Urashima turned his face toward the land and saw again the mountains and the bay he knew so well. They came to the beach, and he stepped ashore.

"Remember," said the turtle. "Do not open the box."

"I will remember," Urashima said.

He walked across the sands and took the path that led to his home. But as he looked around, he was filled with a strange fear. The trees somehow looked different. So did the houses. And he didn't recognize anyone he saw. When he reached his own house, somehow it too looked different. Only the little stream in the garden and a few stepping-stones were the same.

He called: "Mother! Father!" An old man opened the door.

"Who are you?" asked Urashima. "And where are my mother and father? And what has happened to our house? Everything has changed. It is only a matter of days since I left. Only three days since I, Urashima Taro, lived here."

"This is my house," said the old man, "and it was my father's house and my father's father's before him. But I have heard that a man called Urashima Taro once lived here. The story goes that one day he went fishing and didn't return, and then, not long after, his parents died of sorrow. But that was over three hundred years ago."

Urashima shook his head. How could it be that his mother and father, and all of his friends too, had died long, long ago? He thanked the old man and walked slowly back to the shore, where he knelt down on the sands.

Three hundred years, thought Urashima. Three hundred years must be only three days in the Kingdom Under the Sea.

Urashima took the lacquered box the princess had given him out of his pocket and idly played with the red silk cord. And, little by little, the cord came undone. Then, without thinking what he was doing, he opened the first box: Three soft wisps of smoke swirled out and curled around him. Whereupon the handsome youth became an old, old man.

Urashima opened the second box: This one held a mirror. He looked at his reflection and saw that his hair was gray and his face was wrinkled. Then he opened the third box: A crane's feather drifted out, brushed

across his face, and settled on his head. And with that, the old man changed into a bird—a beautiful, elegant crane.

And the crane flew up over the mountains and circled above the sea. He looked down, and there he saw a turtle floating on the waves, close to the shore. The turtle looked up, and she saw the crane. And she knew then that her husband, Urashima Taro, would never, ever return to the kingdom and palace of the Dragon King Under the Sea.

Japanese

✦ *Unanana and the* ✦
Enormous One-Tusked Elephant

Here is a story—a story about Unanana, who one day decided to build a house for herself and her two children, a little boy and a little girl. She built her house, and she built it well. *But* she built the house in the middle of a wide road, and that road was the animals' road through the bush.

Everyone said, "You can't live there. That is the elephants' road . . . the leopards' road . . . the antelopes' road. All the animals use that road. It is a dangerous place."

But Unanana replied, "This is a good place to live. I am Unanana, and I am not afraid."

Now, Unanana's two children were beautiful. *Everyone* who saw them said, "Unanana, you have remarkably beautiful children."

And she always answered, "That is true. They are beautiful, and I love them better than anything in the world."

One morning Unanana had to go into the bush to collect firewood, so she asked the children's big cousin, who was staying with them for a few days, to look after her little boy and little girl. And then, while Unanana went off into the bush, the three cousins went out and played together on the road.

Not long after, a shy gentle-eyed antelope came leaping down the road. When she saw the children, she asked, "Whose children are those?"

And Big Cousin answered, "They are Unanana's children."

"Oh!" said the antelope. "They are beautiful, beautiful children!" And she went on her way.

A little while later, a bold yellow-eyed leopard came prowling down the road. When she saw the children, she asked, "Whose children are those?"

And Big Cousin answered, "They are Unanana's children."

"Oh!" said the leopard. "They are beautiful, beautiful children!" And she too went on her way.

A little while later, an enormous one-tusked elephant came trampling down the road. When he saw the children, he asked, "Whose children are those?"

And Big Cousin answered, "They are Unanana's children."

"Au! Au!" trumpeted the elephant. "They are beautiful, beautiful children! *But* they are playing in the middle of MY road!"

And—next thing—he stretched out his long trunk, picked up the little boy, and swooshed him right into his mouth. *Gulp! gulp!* He swallowed him whole. Then he stretched out his long trunk again, picked up the little girl, and swooshed her right into his mouth. *Gulp! gulp!* He swallowed her whole. And, yet again, he stretched out that long trunk. But Big Cousin wasn't there. Fast, *very fast*, she had run into the house and shut the door behind her.

And so, swinging his long stretchy trunk from side to side, the enormous one-tusked elephant went on trampling down the road.

When Unanana came home with the firewood, the first thing she noticed was that her children were not outside playing. She went into the house, and there was Big Cousin, hunched up in a corner, crying.

"Where are my beautiful children?" asked Unanana.

"They have been taken by an enormous one-tusked elephant," said Big Cousin.

"What did he do with them?" asked Unanana.

"He ate them," answered Big Cousin.

"Did he swallow them whole?" asked Unanana.

"I don't know," answered Big Cousin.

Then Unanana ground some maize, mixed it with milk, and cooked a delicious creamy porridge in a big pot. When the porridge had cooled, she put the pot on her head, picked up a big sharp knife, and set off.

She marched down the animals' road, and she marched and she marched, until she met a shy gentle-eyed antelope.

"Good mother antelope," said Unanana, "where can I find the enormous one-tusked elephant that has eaten my beautiful children?"

The antelope said, "You must go and go and keep on going until you come to the place of tall trees and white stones."

So Unanana marched down the animals' road, and she marched and she marched, until she met a bold yellow-eyed leopard.

"Good mother leopard," she said, "where can I find the enormous one-tusked elephant that has eaten my beautiful children?"

The leopard said, "You must go and go and keep on going until you come to the place of tall trees and white stones."

So Unanana marched down the animals' road, and she marched and she marched, until she saw an enormous one-tusked elephant lying under some tall trees in a place where there were white stones all around.

Unanana marched up to the elephant and said, "Are you the elephant that ate my beautiful children?"

The elephant answered, "No, I am not the one! Go and go and keep on going, and you will find the elephant."

Unanana shouted, *"Are you the elephant that ate my beautiful children?"*

The elephant said, "No, of course I am not the one! Go and go and keep on going, and you will find the elephant."

Then Unanana bellowed, "ARE YOU THE ELEPHANT THAT ATE MY BEAUTIFUL CHILDREN?"

And the elephant, still lying on the ground, stretched out his long trunk, picked up Unanana, and swooshed her into his mouth. *Gulp! gulp!* He swallowed her whole, together with the big sharp knife and the cooking pot full of delicious creamy porridge.

When Unanana got inside the elephant, she *was* surprised. The place was full of dogs, goats, cattle, and a whole lot of people—all just sitting there, slumpish and feeling sorry for themselves.

But Unanana didn't sit down and feel sorry for herself. She marched up, down, around and around inside the elephant until—*such great happiness!*—she found her two beautiful children sitting right next to each other, holding hands.

"Have you had anything to eat?" she asked.

"No," they replied. "And we are very hungry."

"Well," said Unanana, "I have brought you some delicious creamy porridge."

By the time the children had eaten all the porridge they could, every single person and animal inside the elephant had jumped up and gathered around Unanana. They too were very hungry. So she shared the rest of the porridge; there was some for everyone and plenty more besides.

Now, what with Unanana marching up and down and with the people and animals all jumping up and gathering around her, the elephant began to feel uncomfortable.

"Stop moving around down there!" he shouted. "You're giving me a bellyache."

Unanana said, "Stop moving, indeed! Come on, everybody, let's dance!"

So then the dogs, the goats, the cattle, and all the people began to dance.

"Au! Au!" trumpeted the elephant. Now his bellyache was even worse. "Au! Au! Au! Stop dancing down there!"

But they danced and danced.

The elephant thought to himself, From the moment I swallowed that woman, I haven't had any peace! This is too much! So he shouted, "Get out, all of you! Get out!"

"And how can we get out?" Unanana called back.

"Any way you like!" shouted the elephant. "That's how!"

Then Unanana said, "There is only one way."

And she took her big sharp knife and cut a doorway in the side of the elephant.

Out skipped the dogs and the goats and the cattle, barking and bleating and mooing; and then out skipped the people, including Unanana's two beautiful children, laughing. They were all so glad to see the grass and the trees and the sky again.

42 MAGICAL TALES FROM MANY LANDS

The animals thanked Unanana for saving them and hurried home. The people thanked her, too. But, before hurrying home, they all promised to come and visit her one day at her house in the middle of the animals' road.

Meanwhile, the enormous one-tusked elephant just lay there. Even though he had a wound in his side, he was glad to see the animals and the people—and most especially Unanana!—hurrying away. They had given him such a terrible bellyache!

When Unanana and her two children reached home and Big Cousin saw them—*such great happiness!*—Unanana immediately ground some maize and cooked another pot of delicious creamy porridge. Then they all sat down together and ate it.

And did it taste good.

From then on, it was never quiet at Unanana's house, because the people she had met inside the elephant, and even their relatives, all came to visit her. Every time they came, they brought presents—a cow or a goat, something like that. And so Unanana and her two beautiful children became rich.

But they still lived in their house in the middle of the animals' road. Unanana liked it there. And the enormous one-tusked elephant? He never came trampling down that road again.

South African (Zulu)

✦ Kate Crackernuts ✦

Long, long ago, there lived a bonny princess whose name was Kate. Now, it happened that her mother died, and when her father married again, the new queen already had a daughter of her own, whose name also was Kate. So there they were—two Kates in the same family. And it would have been confusing if it wasn't that the king's Kate was by far the bonnier of the two. Nearly everyone called her Bonny Kate, while the queen's daughter they called Kate. Just plain Kate.

Right from the start, the two Kates were friends and loved each other like true sisters. But the queen was bitterly jealous that the king's daughter was bonnier than her own. One day she could bear it no longer and went to see the hen-wife, an old witch who kept a flock of hens not far from the castle gates. The queen asked her to cast a spell on the king's daughter that would spoil the beauty of Bonny Kate.

"Send the lassie to me," said the hen-wife, "without a bite to eat or a drop to drink, and I'll soon hash up her bonny face."

Early next morning, the queen sent the king's daughter to the hen-wife to fetch a basket of eggs for breakfast. But on her way through the kitchen, Bonny Kate saw some oatcakes on the table, so she picked one up and ate it as she walked along.

When she came to the hen-wife's house and asked for the eggs, the hen-wife said, "Lift the lid off that pot there and see what you can see."

Bonny Kate lifted the lid off the black pot that hung over the fire, and a cloud of steam rose up. A cloud of steam and nothing more.

And the hen-wife cried, "Go home to the queen and tell her to keep her larder door better locked!"

Well, the next morning Bonny Kate was sent once again to fetch a basket of eggs. She went through the kitchen, and the table was bare. She tried the larder, and the door was locked. But as she walked along the road, she saw an old man picking peas. Being a friendly lass, she stopped for a chat and admired his peas. The old man gave her a handful of pods, and off she went, munching peas.

Again she came to the hen-wife's house and asked for the eggs, and again the hen-wife said, "Lift the lid off that pot there and see what you can see."

So Bonny Kate lifted the lid off the black pot, and a cloud of steam rose up. A cloud of steam and nothing more.

And the hen-wife cried, "Go home to the queen and tell her that if she wants something done, she must come herself!"

Scottish

Well, the next morning the queen herself woke Bonny Kate and didn't let her out of her sight. Not for one single moment. And she kept beside her every step of the way to the hen-wife's house.

When they got there, once again the hen-wife said, "Now, lift the lid off that pot there and see what you can see."

Bonny Kate lifted the lid, and a sheep's head rose up out of the pot and jumped onto her shoulders and covered her own bonny head entirely. So there she was with a sheep's head instead of her own.

Now the queen was satisfied.

But the other Kate, the queen's own daughter, was very angry when she saw what had happened. "We can no longer stay here!" she said to Bonny Kate. "Who knows what may befall you next!" So she took a fine linen cloth, wrapped it around her sister's head, and took her by the hand. Together they set out to seek their fortune.

They walked far, they walked farther than far, until they came at last to another kingdom. Kate went boldly to the king's castle and found

work as a kitchen maid, saying her sister was sick; in return, she and her sick sister were given food and allowed to sleep in a small room in the attic.

Now, the king had two sons, and the elder of the two was ill. No one knew what ailed him. Day in, day out, he lay in bed, sleeping. The strange thing was that anyone who sat to watch over him at night disappeared and was never seen or heard from again. So a time came when there was no one left brave enough to sit with the prince at night.

Now, there was not much Kate was afraid of. When she heard about the trouble, she said, "I'll do that. For a bag full of silver, I'll sit with the prince."

The king agreed.

So that night Kate sat with the sleeping prince. All went well until midnight. As soon as the castle clock struck twelve, the prince rose from his bed as if in a daze and dressed himself. Then off he went, down the stairs, out the front door, and into the stable, with Kate following at his heels. He saddled his horse, called his hound, and mounted. And Kate leaped lightly up behind him.

Away they rode, with the hound running alongside. They came to a wood of close-growing hazel, and as they wound in and out among the trees, Kate picked hazelnuts from the branches and filled her apron pockets with them. They rode on until they came to a green hill, and then the prince called out, "Open, open, green hill, and let the young prince in with his horse and hound."

"And," added Kate, "his fair lady behind him."

Then a door opened in the hillside, and they went through and entered a brightly lit hall full of handsome people dancing to the liveliest, most toe-tapping music Kate had ever heard.

Now, as soon as they were inside, Kate slipped off the horse and hid among the shadows near the door. Immediately some beautiful ladies surrounded the prince and led him off to dance. He danced with each in turn and did not rest for a moment. He danced and danced.

Then Kate knew that she was in the hall of the fairy folk, and she knew too that she must be careful, for if they caught her spying on them, they would never, ever let her go. So she drew back and hid herself in

the deepest, darkest shadows she could find.

After a while, she happened to notice a fairy child playing with a silver wand, and then she heard one of the fairy women say, "You take care of that wand. Three strokes from it, just three, would make the poor wee lassie with the sheep's head as bonny as ever she was!"

So then Kate took some hazelnuts out of her pockets and rolled them toward the fairy child. She rolled them and rolled them until the child dropped the wand and chased after the nuts. Quickly Kate crept forward, snatched up the wand, and hid it under her apron.

After that, the cock crowed. The prince came and mounted his horse, and Kate leaped lightly up behind him. They rode back to the castle, the hound again running alongside.

When the horse was stabled, and the prince once more fast asleep in his bed, Kate sat down by the fire and cracked some nuts and ate them.

In the morning the king, the queen, and the prince's younger brother came into the room. Kate told them that the prince had had a good night. That was all she said. When the king asked her to watch over his son for a second night, she told him, "I'll do that. For a bag full of gold, I'll sit with the prince." And the king agreed.

Now, as soon as they had left, Kate took the wand and hurried up to the attic room she shared with her sister. She touched Bonny Kate three times with the wand, and there and then the sheep's head disappeared and her sister was as bonny as ever she was!

The next night came, and the same things happened as before. When the clock struck twelve, the prince rose from his bed, dressed, went down the stairs and out the front door, saddled his horse, and called his hound. He mounted, and Kate leaped up behind him. When they took the winding path through the woods, Kate again filled her apron pockets with hazelnuts. And when they came to the green hill, the prince again said, "Open, open, green hill, and let the young prince in with his horse and hound."

"And," added Kate, "his fair lady behind him."

The door swung open, and they entered the magnificent hall where the dancers danced and the fiddlers played. Again Kate hid in the shadows while the prince danced without resting.

After a while, Kate noticed a fairy child playing with a white bird, chasing it and catching it. Then she heard one of the fairy women say, "You take care of that bird. Three bites of it, just three, would set the prince free from our fairy enchantment and make him as well as ever he was."

So Kate took some hazelnuts out of her pockets and rolled them toward the child. She rolled them and rolled them until the child let go of the bird and chased after them. Quickly Kate crept forward and snatched up the bird and hid it under her apron.

Then the cock crowed, the prince mounted his horse, and Kate leaped up behind him. And they were off, back to the palace, with the hound running alongside.

When the horse was in the stable and the prince once more fast asleep in his bed, Kate killed and plucked the bird and hung it over the fire to roast. Before long, a rich, savory smell filled the room.

The prince stirred and opened his eyes. "Oh!" he said. "I'd like a taste of that bird!" So Kate gave him a bite.

The prince rose up on his elbow, and by and by he said, "Oh! I'd like another taste of that bird!" So Kate gave him a second bite.

Now he sat up in bed, and by and by he said, "Oh! If only I could have another taste of that bird!" So Kate gave him a third bite.

Then the prince leaped from his bed, fit and well as ever he was. In the morning, when the king, the queen, and the younger brother came, they found Kate and the prince sitting by the fire, cracking nuts and eating them, rattling on about this and that, just like old friends.

The king and queen were so happy! The king said to Kate, "I promised you a bag full of silver and a bag full of gold, and they shall be yours. But that is not enough, for you have done more than watch over my

son. You have healed him. So you may ask for anything you wish."

"Anything?" asked Kate.

"Yes, anything I have is yours," replied the king.

"Then," said Kate, "what I'd like best of all is to marry the prince!"

There, she had said it! Kate was not shy.

The prince was more than willing. He was eager to marry this bright-eyed, lively Kate.

Not long after that, the prince's younger brother said that he wanted to marry the other Kate, the bonny sister who had been sick. So, in the end, there was a double wedding. The two Kates married the two brothers.

There they were again—two Kates in the same family. And it would

have been confusing, but the prince who had been sick said that he was going to call his Kate *Kate Crackernuts* because it was while they sat by the fire cracking hazelnuts that he had first come to know her and love her.

And Kate Crackernuts liked her new name. It made her smile.

Scottish

✦ The King Who Wanted ✦
to Touch the Moon

Long ago there lived a king who always had to have his own way. Everyone had to do exactly what he said. Immediately. No back talk, no arguing.

Well, one night this king looked out the window and saw the silvery moon riding high in the sky, and then and there he wanted to reach out and touch it. But even he couldn't do that. So he thought about it and thought about it. Night and day he thought about it. At last he worked out a way that he could touch the moon. He would have a tall, tall tower built that reached to the sky, and then he would climb to the top and touch the moon.

So he ordered the royal carpenter to build the tower.

The carpenter shook his head. "A tower so tall that it reaches right to the moon? Your Majesty, it is not possible. It can't be done."

"Can't!" shouted the king. "There's no such word as *can't* in this kingdom. Come back tomorrow morning, first thing, and tell me exactly how you are going to build my tower."

The carpenter did some hard thinking, and in the end he worked out a way to build a tall tower.

The next morning he went to the king and said, "Your Majesty, the way to build the tower is to pile up lots of strong wooden chests, one on top of the other, hundreds and thousands of them, until they reach the sky."

Now, the king liked this idea. So he ordered his subjects to search their homes and bring all their strong chests to the palace. Immediately. And if anyone refused? Well, there was plenty of room in the royal prisons.

So, of course, the people brought their chests to the king. And there were all kinds of chests—big and small, carved and polished, painted and plain.

Then the carpenter and his assistants set to work. They laid chest upon chest, one on top of the other, up and up; and before long, a tall tower stood outside the palace. But when all the chests had been used, the tower did not even reach to the clouds.

So the king said to the carpenter, "Make more chests!"

Wood was found, and the carpenter and his assistants sawed and hammered and made more chests. They laid them one on top of the other, up and up. But when all the chests had been used, the tower reached only to the clouds.

"Make more chests!" said the king to the carpenter.

"We have no more wood, your Majesty," the carpenter replied.

"Then cut down all the trees and get more wood," ordered the king.

The carpenter shook his head. "All the trees!" he said. "Oh, no, we can't do that—"

"Did I hear you say *can't?* Have you forgotten there is no such word as *can't* in this kingdom?" demanded the king. "Go and cut down *all* the trees. Immediately."

So all the trees in the kingdom were chopped down—the great ancient trees and the slender saplings, the fruit trees and the nut trees and the

flowering trees—all were cut down and sawed into planks and made into chests. More and more chests. And the chests were laid one on top of the other, up and up. When all the chests had been used, the tower reached beyond the clouds and into the sky.

The king gazed up at the tower and was pleased. "The time has come for me to climb my tall, tall tower and touch the moon," he announced.

Then he began to climb, up, up, and up, until at last he stood at the top of his tall, tall tower. He looked up and he stretched out both his arms, but he could not quite reach the moon. He stood on the tips of

his toes and stretched some more. He was very close. He could *almost* touch the moon. But not quite.

The king shouted down, "Bring up another chest! Just one! One will be enough!"

The carpenter looked around. There were no more chests. And no more wood. And not a single tree in all the land.

So he called out, "Your Majesty, there are no more chests!"

The king shouted back, "Then take one out from the bottom and bring it up here."

The carpenter was astonished. He couldn't take a chest out from the bottom of the pile. Well, could he? Surely the king was not serious!

But the king was shouting again.

"Didn't you hear me? Take one out from the bottom! Immediately!"

The carpenter raised his eyebrows, shrugged his shoulders, and did as he was told. He pulled a chest out from the bottom of the pile.

And you can imagine what happened next. The whole tall tower came tumbling down, king, chests, and more chests, one on top of the other. So that was the end of the king who always had to have his own way and wanted, above everything else, to touch the moon.

Caribbean

✦ *Three Golden Apples* ✦

Once there was a happy king. He had a large kingdom, a lovely queen, and a daughter, Princess Isabelle, who was as beautiful as the day.

But misfortune creeps up from behind, and one night Princess Isabelle fell ill. A great troop of doctors came to the palace to examine her. They stroked their beards and shook their heads. They had no idea what was the matter, so they tried first one remedy and then another. But nothing helped the princess, and as time passed, she began to fade away, until it seemed certain she would die.

The king was beside himself. He was willing to see anyone and try anything, if only he could save his daughter.

One morning an old man came to the palace. "You must find the golden apples," he said to the king.

"Golden apples!" exclaimed the king. "What golden apples?"

"In a far distant corner of the kingdom," said the old man, "there is a garden where wild nightingales sing night and day. In the garden stands an apple tree, all white with blossoms, and on the tree hang nine golden apples. Three of these apples will cure your daughter. Of that I am certain."

Here was good news at last! Straightaway the king ordered his heralds to go and proclaim in every town and village that the man who brought three golden apples and cured Princess Isabelle would be richly rewarded. He could marry the princess and inherit the kingdom!

Now, in a distant corner of the land, there lived a poor peasant and his three sons. All they had was a small house, a cow, some hens, and a garden. But in that garden wild nightingales sang night and day, and there grew an apple tree that was all white with blossoms. And on that tree hung nine golden apples.

As soon as the three brothers heard the king's proclamation, they all wanted to take the apples and try their luck. But the eldest insisted that, since he had been born first, he must go first. So he picked the three biggest apples, put them in a basket, covered them with a clean cloth, and off he went.

He had not gone far when he met an old woman. "What's in your basket, my friend?" she asked.

"Slimy toads!" he answered rudely. "Just slimy toads!"

"And slimy toads they shall be!" replied the old woman.

The eldest brother walked and walked until he reached the palace. When he told the guards that he had three golden apples in his basket, he was taken straight through the corridors and up the steps to where the king and queen sat on their royal thrones.

"Your Majesty," he said, "I have brought you three golden apples."

The king was overjoyed. He lifted the cloth and put his hand in the basket and— Oh! What was this? Three slimy toads!

The king sprang up and gave the lad a hard slap that sent him rolling down the steps—toads, basket, and all!

So the eldest brother trudged home and told his family about his bad luck. Golden apples that had changed into toads!

The second brother was sure he could do better. He picked the three next-biggest apples, put them in a basket, covered them with a clean cloth, and off he went.

He had not gone far when he met the same old woman. "What's in your basket, my friend?" she said.

"Slithery snakes!" he answered rudely. "Just slithery snakes!"

"And slithery snakes they shall be!" replied the old woman.

The second brother walked and walked until he reached the palace. Then he too was taken straight through the corridors and up the steps to where the king and queen sat on their thrones.

"Your Majesty," said the second brother, "I have brought you three golden apples."

The king was once again joyous. He lifted the cloth and put his hand in the basket and— Oh! What was this? Three slithery snakes!

The king jumped up and gave this lad *two* hard slaps that sent him rolling twice as fast down the steps—snakes, basket, and all!

So the second brother trudged home and told his family about his bad luck. Golden apples that had changed into snakes!

Then the youngest brother, who was called Martin, said that it was now his turn to go.

"You—the youngest and smallest!" laughed the eldest brother.

"You think you can do better than us!" scoffed the second.

"I can try," said Martin.

So he picked the three remaining apples from the tree, put them in a basket, and covered them with a clean cloth. Then, with clean clogs on his feet and his best clothes on his back, he was on his way, whistling like a blackbird in spring.

He had not gone far when he met the same old woman. "What's in your basket, my friend?" she said.

"Three golden apples, madame," he answered politely. "Just three golden apples."

"And three golden apples they shall be," she said. "But tell me, what are these apples for?"

"It is said these apples will cure Princess Isabelle," said Martin. "And then I shall be allowed to marry her."

"Marry a princess? Ah—you may need extra help for that," the old woman said. "So take this silver whistle. It may prove useful."

The youngest brother took it and thanked her and dropped the whistle in his pocket. Then he walked and walked, and when he reached the palace, he too was taken straight to the king and queen.

Martin bowed. "Your Majesty," he said, "I have brought you three golden apples."

Now, this time the king was suspicious. And no wonder! He lifted the cloth very slowly and peeked inside the basket.

"Three golden apples!" he exclaimed.

The king seized the basket and was off—striding along to Princess Isabelle's room, with the queen at his heels and Martin and a crowd of royal courtiers behind.

Princess Isabelle ate one golden apple and sighed. She ate a second and sat up in bed. She ate a third and jumped out of bed, well and happy and more beautiful than ever.

"Now I must marry the lad who brought the golden apples," she said.

Martin looked at Princess Isabelle. Yes, he liked the idea of marrying her.

But the king looked at his daughter and thought, A princess is a princess. But a peasant . . . *hmmm* . . . a peasant is only a peasant. So we shall see.

He turned to Martin. "You will have to prove yourself before you can marry my daughter. The princess has one hundred pet hares, which are

kept in my stables. Tomorrow you must take those hares out to graze in the fields and bring them back in the evening—every single one of them."

"It sounds hard," said Martin, "but I can try."

The next morning the king's servants opened the stable doors, and by the time the last hare came leaping out, the first one was out of sight.

It will be impossible to find all of them again, thought Martin, slouching along with his hands in his pockets. And then his fingers touched the whistle. Could it be useful? He took it out and blew a long blast.

Hares came bounding toward him from all sides. Martin counted them—one hundred exactly! His troubles were over. He led the hares out to a big meadow, where they played while he lay in the grass and thought about this and that. When evening came, he blew the whistle and—*forward march!*—off he went, with the hares leaping along behind him.

The king could not believe his eyes when he saw them coming. He counted the hares. Sure enough, there were one hundred exactly.

But the king said, "Before you can marry my daughter, you must look after the hares for a second day."

So the next morning the stable doors were opened, and Martin again set off with the hares.

But the king was crafty and had made some plans. In the afternoon a

woman came riding into the field on a donkey. She wore an old, faded dress, a scarf tied around her head, and clogs on her feet. She looked like a poor peasant, but Martin was not fooled. He recognized the queen's face.

"Please sell me one of your hares," she said. "It would make such a good dinner for my hungry little children."

"The hares are not for sale," said Martin. "But you can earn one."

"And what must I do?"

"Give me three rosy kisses!" he replied.

This was not the sort of thing to ask of a queen. Nor was it the sort of thing for a queen to grant. But this queen wanted one of those hares, so she gave him three quick kisses.

Martin picked up a hare and handed it to her, and she rode off, holding it tightly in her arms. But before she reached the palace gates, he blew

the whistle, and the hare wriggled free and came bounding back to him.

In the evening, Martin again blew his whistle and—*forward march!*—back to the palace he went, with the hares leaping along behind him.

The king did some more careful counting, and sure enough, there were one hundred hares exactly. But the king was determined.

"Before you can marry my daughter, you must look after the hares for a third day," he told Martin.

The next morning Martin went off with the hares yet again. But the crafty king had made more plans, and in the afternoon a man came along, riding on a donkey. He was wearing a patched jacket, torn trousers, a black beret on his head, and clogs on his feet. He looked like a poor peasant, but Martin recognized the face immediately. It was the king himself.

"Sell me one of your hares," he said. "I'll give you a good price."

"The hares are not for sale," answered Martin. "But you can earn one."

"And what must I do?"

"Well," said Martin, "I shall cut a branch off this wild rosebush. Then you must bend over, and I will give you three whacks!"

Now, this was *definitely* not the sort of thing to ask of a king. Yet the king did want one of those hares. So he climbed down from the donkey and bent over, and Martin gave him three whacks—one, two, three.

Then the king mounted the donkey, and Martin handed him a hare. The king held that hare very tightly as he rode off. But before he could reach the palace gates, Martin blew the whistle, and the hare wriggled free and came bounding back to him.

When evening came, the lad blew his whistle once more and—*forward march!*—back to the palace went Martin, with the hares leaping along behind him.

And when the king did his counting, all one hundred hares were there yet again. "Humph!" he grumbled. "Come to the palace tomorrow, and we shall see what is what."

The next morning Martin presented himself at the palace. The king and the queen and Princess Isabelle sat on their royal thrones, and the courtiers were gathered below them. Martin thought that now, at last, he had won the princess.

But no! The king said, "Before you can marry my daughter, you must prove that you have both wit and wisdom. You must talk and keep on talking until you have told me a whole sackful of interesting truths. And only when *I* say that the sack is full may you stop talking and marry her."

Martin grinned. He could think of some very good truths that would help fill that sack.

"Here is the first truth," he began. "One day when I was guarding Princess Isabelle's pet hares, the queen came along. She was dressed like a peasant and riding a donkey. And—would you believe it?—she wanted a hare. She wanted it so much that she gave me—"

"No!" cried the king. "No! No! No! I won't listen!"

"The queen gave me three kisses for one hare!"

There. The king couldn't say that was a lie.

"Now, the next day when I was guarding the hares," said Martin, "the king came along. He was dressed like a peasant and riding a donkey. And—would you believe it?—he too wanted a hare—"

"Oh! Don't tell!" cried the king.

"And he wanted it so much that he—"

"That's enough!"

"His Royal Majesty bent—"

"Stop! Stop!"

"He bent over, and I—"

"Stop! You have said enough! The sack is full! Completely full! You may marry my daughter!"

And so the next day Martin married Princess Isabelle, who you can be sure was very happy, for she loved him even though he was a peasant lad and she was a princess.

French

✦ The Magic Fruit ✦

In the time long ago when great and marvelous magicians lived on earth, Coniraya was the greatest of all. With his hollow stick, he could turn mountains into flatlands. He could make deserts run with rivers. He could make big, powerful magic. Yet sometimes, because he liked jokes and pranks, Coniraya just looked around and made mischief.

Now, while Coniraya was the greatest among magicians, there was a young woman called Cavillaca who was the most beautiful. She was so beautiful, in fact, that every young man, as soon as he saw her, wanted to marry her. But Cavillaca was proud, and she thought that no living man was handsome enough or powerful enough for her. And so she refused to marry.

One day when Coniraya was walking about the world disguised as a

poor peasant, he saw Cavillaca sitting under a tree, weaving. Then he, like everyone else, wanted to marry her.

"Greetings, beautiful Cavillaca," said Coniraya.

But Cavillaca kept her eyes on her weaving.

So Coniraya thought up some mischief. The next moment, there he was—a large bird with glorious rainbow-colored feathers. He spread his wide wings and flew up to a branch of the tree that stretched out above Cavillaca. He began to sing.

But Cavillaca only kept her eyes on her weaving.

Coniraya thought up some more mischief. He conjured up a fruit. It was shiny and golden, flushed with a soft rosy pink. He hid strong magic inside the fruit and dropped it straight down into Cavillaca's lap.

Well, the fruit looked so lovely, she had to pick it up. It smelled so good, she had to bite into it. And the fruit tasted so delicious, she had to eat it to the last juicy mouthful.

Cavillaca did not guess that it was a magic fruit.

Months passed. Then, because of the magic fruit, Cavillaca had a son. He was a beautiful, happy baby, and she loved him with a great love.

But she kept wondering who had made magic and given her this baby, how it had been done, and when. Cavillaca thought about it and thought about it; and when the baby was almost a year old and could crawl, she decided that she would find out who the father of her beautiful child was, and marry him. Because, without doubt, he must be both exceedingly powerful and exceedingly handsome. So she summoned the great magicians to a meeting.

Of course, they all came dressed in their most splendid robes, hoping that Cavillaca would notice them. All except for Coniraya, that is, who once again was dressed in the torn, shabby clothes of a poor peasant.

The meeting began. Cavillaca stood, proud and beautiful, with her baby in her arms. "Until this time I have always refused to marry," she told the magicians, "but now I solemnly promise that I will marry the father of my son if he will make himself known to me."

No one spoke. Certainly not the mischief maker Coniraya.

"If you will not speak, then my son shall tell me," said Cavillaca. "He will know his father and go to him."

She put the baby on the ground, and immediately he was off, crawling eagerly, straight toward the peasant. When the baby reached the peasant's feet, he looked up and stretched out his arms.

Proud Cavillaca was angry.

"A poor peasant! No, I will *not* marry a poor peasant!" she cried, running to the baby and sweeping him up in her arms. "Though I have given my promise," she said, "I will *never* marry him. I would rather die."

And, clasping her son close, she ran off.

"Stop!" Coniraya called out. "Stop! Things are not as they seem!"

But she would not listen and ran on.

Then Coniraya struck the ground with his hollow stick. The next moment, there he stood, dressed in magnificent robes, dazzling and golden.

"Beautiful Cavillaca, look back. Turn your eyes toward me and see how handsome and splendid I have become," the great magician called.

But Cavillaca ran on as before.

And now Coniraya was afraid of beautiful Cavillaca's stubborn pride and sorry for his own mischief making. He quickly ran after her.

But she heard him coming and gathered together her own powerful magic. She hid herself from him and ran faster, ever faster.

Though he could not tell where she had gone, Coniraya was determined to find her. As he ran, he asked everyone he met—people and animals both—if they had seen her. But no one had. At last, good fortune came. He met the Condor, who had seen her and was able to show him the way.

Coniraya thanked the Condor with a blessing. "I give you power to fly over the valleys and wild places and to eat where you will," he said. "A curse be on those who kill the Condor."

More good fortune came. Coniraya met the Falcon, who had also seen Cavillaca and was able to show him the way.

Coniraya blessed the Falcon. "I give you power to soar above the mountains," he said. "In song and dance the Indian shall always praise the Falcon."

On he ran, and again good fortune came. He met the Puma, who was also able to show him the way.

Coniraya blessed the Puma. "I give you power over all other living creatures," he said. "At all times the Indian shall honor the Puma."

Coniraya ran on and came to the sea, and at last he saw Cavillaca for himself. She was running across the shore. He called to her, but she would not look back.

Clasping her baby in her arms and gathering together all her magic powers, she plunged into the sea. The next moment, there was no beautiful Cavillaca and no baby. They were gone.

In their place stood two rocks, a large one and a small one close beside it. Two rocks and the waves that gently lapped against them—that was all.

Peruvian (Inca)

✦ Seven Clever Brothers ✦

Once upon a time a king and a queen had seven sons, each one born on a different day of the week. The king and queen named each son after the day on which he was born. The eldest was called Sunday, the next Monday, the one after that Tuesday, and so on, all the way to the youngest, who was called Saturday. And when those princes grew up, they were all clever, all handsome, and all seven of them good friends.

Now, one day the brothers decided the time had come for them to leave home and see the world. But when they told the king, he said, "You can all go except Saturday. I must keep one of my sons with me, and I shall keep Saturday, for he is the youngest and smallest."

But Saturday wanted to go with his brothers. He pleaded with his father and wouldn't keep quiet. In the end, the king relented.

"Only promise me one thing," said the king to all his sons. "Whatever happens, you will never quarrel, but always stay friends, as brothers should." The brothers promised. They could think of no reason why they should ever want to quarrel.

The next day they set off. They walked for seven days under a hot sun, until they came to a place where seven roads lay before them. Each brother wanted to choose a different road.

Sunday, the eldest, said, "Let us not quarrel. Let us each take our own road, go our separate ways, and then meet here again one year from today."

So each brother strode off down the road he chose. Exactly one year later, they all met again at the same place. Immediately they began talking, the way brothers do.

Saturday, the youngest, said to the eldest, "Well, Sunday, what's the news? What did you find in the big world?"

"Oh! I found something marvelous!" said Sunday. "A pair of spectacles!"

"Nothing so marvelous about that," Saturday remarked.

"Isn't there now? Well, if you put these spectacles on your nose, little brother, you can see anything that's happening up to five hundred miles away."

"Now, that is something!" agreed Monday, and his brothers nodded their heads. "But—guess what? I also found something marvelous. An old fiddle!"

Saturday shrugged his shoulders. "Is that all?"

"Ah—but strangers who hear me play this fiddle quickly fall asleep," explained Monday.

"That could be useful and amusing," said Tuesday. "Now, don't laugh, and I'll tell you what I've learned. I can take things out of anyone's pocket, even out of their hands, so lightly they don't notice."

"So you're a pickpocket! Amazing!" cried Wednesday. "But I think I too can surprise you. I found a coat. And this coat has a pocket. And I can put *anything* into this pocket—it doesn't matter how big. It always fits."

"That's something to marvel at!" exclaimed Thursday. "All I have is a little twig from an oak tree. But if I swish it to and fro, it will send big, thick oak cudgels flying through the air to beat my enemies. One or a hundred. This twig can manage anything!"

"That could be useful in battle," said Friday. "As for me, I've learned to shoot with a bow and arrow. I can hit anything. Even a seed in a bird's beak, miles away!"

"So you're an expert shot!" said Saturday. "Now, me, I've learned to do some throwing and catching. I can throw anything with my right hand, even a heavy millstone, as high as I like, and catch it in my left hand."

"Show us, little brother!" said Sunday. "Show us!"

"You will have to wait and see," replied Saturday.

Then, after a lot more talking, the brothers decided that they would travel together for a while before returning home. So they drew lots to decide which road to take, and off they went.

They walked and walked until they came to a strange, silent city, all draped in black. Everyone there looked sad. It seemed that the king's only daughter had vanished; no one knew where she was or who had taken her.

When the brothers heard this, they glanced at each other, all thinking the same thing. Perhaps *they* could find the princess. So they went to the king and offered to try.

The king was pleased. "The one who finds my daughter can have half my kingdom, half my treasure, half of all I possess, *and* marry my daughter, provided she is willing," he said.

Then Sunday went to the window and put on his spectacles. "I see a dark, dismal castle," he told the others. "And in it there is an old man with a face the color of parchment, long gray hair, and robes of black and gold. Next to him stands a beautiful maiden whose eyes are filled with tears."

"Tell me," said the king. "What does she look like?"

"There is something curious," said Sunday. "On her left hand she has six fingers."

"Then she is indeed my daughter," said the king. "And the man is the old sorcerer who wanted to marry her. Alas, you will not be able to save her, for he is a clever, wily magician."

"Trust us," said Sunday. "We shall find her and bring her back."

The seven brothers set off, with Sunday showing them the way. They walked and walked until at last they came to the dark, dismal castle. They gave seven loud knocks at the door and told the servant who opened it that they were seven princes who had come to see the sorcerer.

"He is about to celebrate his marriage," said the servant.

"Then we are just in time," Monday told him. "We have come to play music at the wedding feast."

The brothers were escorted to a splendid hall. And there, surrounded by wedding guests, stood the sorcerer, holding a sad-faced maiden firmly by the hand.

Monday tucked his fiddle under his chin and played, and everyone, except for the brothers themselves, closed their eyes and fell asleep. Then Tuesday crept across the room, released the princess from the sorcerer's grasp, and gave her to Wednesday. Wednesday slipped her into his coat pocket—where she fit just perfectly.

The brothers hurried off. They passed the servants in the corridors and the guards outside. But no one stopped them, for no one guessed that Wednesday carried the princess in his pocket.

Not long after, the sorcerer woke up. He immediately knew what had happened and ordered a company of soldiers to ride out and capture the princess and the seven princes.

Now, the brothers had not gone far when, at the sound of horses' hooves, they looked back and saw the soldiers galloping toward them. So Thursday took out his little twig and swished it to and fro. The next moment hundreds of oak cudgels went flying through the air and proceeded to beat those soldiers until the men were so frightened they turned around and rode back to the castle.

Then the brothers walked and walked under a hot sun until they had to sit down beneath a large, shady tree and rest. Wednesday thought it was now safe to take the princess out of his pocket.

Well, when she woke up and opened her eyes, she was more than a little surprised to find herself under a tree surrounded by seven young men. But when the brothers told her who they were and how they had saved her, she was so grateful that she thanked them over and over again. Then they all talked together in a friendly fashion until, one after the other, they fell asleep.

Now, when the soldiers returned to the castle and told the sorcerer about the oak cudgels, he realized that recapturing the princess was something he must do himself. So he began to shiver all over and changed into an enormous black vulture. He spread his wings and flew up into the sky, scanning to the north and south, to the east and west. And

finally he saw the brothers and the princess asleep under a tree. So he swooped down and seized the princess in his beak and flew off.

She called out as loudly as she could, and the brothers woke up. They saw the vulture high in the sky, with the princess in his beak. Friday jumped to his feet, inserted an arrow into his bow, took aim, and hit the vulture in the eye.

The vulture let go of the princess, and she fell down . . . down . . . down . . . toward the earth. But Saturday was quick. He stretched out his left arm, opened his hand, and caught her.

Then the princess and the seven brothers set off together, taking the road back to her father's palace. But, alas, on the way the brothers, those seven brothers who had always been friends, started to quarrel. The princess was so beautiful that they all wanted to marry her.

Sunday said, "If I hadn't looked through my spectacles, we wouldn't have found out where she was. So she should be mine."

"Yes," said Monday, "but if I hadn't played my fiddle and put everyone to sleep, we never could have rescued her."

"But who was the one who released her from the sorcerer's hand so carefully that no one woke?" asked Tuesday.

"But if I hadn't hidden her in my coat pocket, the guards and servants would have seen her as we left," declared Wednesday. "So she surely belongs to me."

"All quite true," agreed Thursday. "But if I had not used my little twig and beaten the soldiers, they would have captured her again."

"Still," said Friday, "if I hadn't shot the vulture and killed him, what then?"

"You have all had your say," Saturday told them. "So now be good enough to listen to me. If I had not caught the princess as she fell from the sky, she would have died, true enough. But still, we are all fools for quarreling. We promised our father that we would always stay friends. And anyway, what about the princess? What about her feelings? Maybe she won't want to marry any of us!"

Saturday turned to the princess, who was walking behind them. He saw there was a smile on her face, for she had heard every word!

"Without the help of all seven of you, I would not be standing here," she said. "I am grateful to all of you, but I have made my choice. I wish to marry Saturday, the youngest and smallest, because when I was falling helpless from the sky and most afraid, he caught me and held me safe. Without Saturday, I would have died."

So the princess herself settled it.

Now, when they came at last to the palace, the king welcomed them with open arms, and celebrations began. Trumpets sounded, cannons boomed, and flags flew from every tower and steeple.

A great and glorious wedding took place, as Saturday married the princess. And *then* there were more celebrations!

After the wedding, the king offered the seven brothers half of all that he had—his kingdom and his treasures—as a reward for finding and saving his daughter. But Saturday said that since he had married the princess, everything should be given to his brothers. The princess was reward enough. So the six brothers shared everything between them. And there were no quarrels, not even a small one.

Then the seven princes, and the princess with them, traveled back to their own kingdom, where the king, their father, was happy and proud when he saw them and heard their news.

"My sons, you are such clever, handsome young men, and besides that, good friends," he said to them. "For what more can I ask? There is only one thing I lack. A daughter. And now you have brought me one, the beautiful princess, wife of my youngest son, Saturday."

And the celebrations began all over again!

Jewish

✦ The Prince ✦
and the Flying Carpet

There was once a prince who was so fond of hunting that he rode out every day in search of game. But one day he seemed to have no luck, and by late afternoon, he had still caught nothing. So he rode on until he came to a dark jungle where he had never been before. There he saw a flock of bright parrots, perched in the trees. The prince lifted his bow and took aim.

But before he could release the arrow, there was a whirl and flurry of feathers. The parrots flew up and away, leaving but one bird still sitting there.

"Do not shoot me!" cried the bird. "I am the raja of all parrots. I am the one who can tell you about Princess Maya."

The prince lowered his bow and approached the bird. "Princess Maya!" he exclaimed. "Who is Princess Maya?"

"Ahhh . . . the beautiful Princess Maya," crooned the bird. "What can I say? She is radiant as the moon, warm and gentle as the evening sun. In this great world she is beyond compare."

"Where does she live?" inquired the prince. "How can I find her?"

"Go forward, ever forward," replied the parrot, "through dark jungles and across wide plains, and you will find her."

As the prince rode home, he made up his mind to find the beautiful Princess Maya, even if he had to search the whole wide world.

But when he told his mother and father about his plans, they were sad. He was their only child, their golden treasure, and they did not want to lose him. But the prince had decided to go, and he would not change his mind.

The very next morning he dressed in his finest clothes, took his bow

and arrows and some food for the journey, mounted his favorite horse, and set off.

Well, he rode until he came to the dark jungle where he had seen the parrots. And then he rode on from there and came to a wide plain, and still he rode forward. Soon he passed into another dark jungle, and then, all of a sudden, he heard loud, angry voices from a nearby clearing. Quietly he approached the clearing and saw three demons, three small,

sharp-eyed, wicked-looking demons, all bunched around a bag, a stick, and an ancient carpet lying on the ground.

"What is the matter?" asked the prince.

One of the demons pointed at the things on the ground and said, "Our master died and left us these. And I want *all* of them!"

"So do I!" shouted the second demon.

"Me too!" shouted the third.

"A bag, a stick, and an ancient carpet," remarked the prince with surprise. "They're not worth quarreling about."

"Not worth quarreling about!" the first demon squalled out, nearly cracking his throat. "Not worth quarreling about! Why, that bag will give you anything you ask for. And that stick will beat your enemies, and—see the rope coiled around it?—that will tie them up so they can't escape. As for the carpet, it will take you wherever you want to go."

"Is that so?" said the prince. And then he did some quick thinking. "Maybe I could settle your quarrel. Let me shoot three arrows into the air. The first one of you to find an arrow and bring it back can have all the treasures."

"Yes!" "A good idea!" "Let's do that!" the demons shouted, each one certain *he* was the fastest runner, each one certain *he* would win.

So the prince let fly three arrows, and off the quarrelsome trio ran, full pelt. Then he jumped down from his horse and turned it around to

face the way they had come. "Lift your fine hooves, my lovely horse," he said. "Make haste and gallop home!" And off went the horse.

Then the prince picked up the stick and the bag, unrolled the carpet, and sat down on it, cross-legged. "Carpet!" he commanded. "Take me to the city where Princess Maya dwells!"

The carpet rose up in the air until it was higher than the trees. Then, smooth and steady, it flew over the dark jungles and plains until it came to the edge of a great city. Whereupon it gently floated down.

As soon as the carpet touched the ground, the prince stood up, stretched himself, and looked around. He rolled up the carpet, and, with the bag over his shoulder, the carpet tucked under his arm, and the stick in his hand, he strode off into the city.

The first person he met was an old woman. "Is this the city where Princess Maya lives?" the prince asked her.

"Indeed it is," she told him.

"How can I find her?" he asked.

"Every evening," the old woman replied, "the princess comes and sits upon the palace roof for one whole hour, lighting the city with her beauty."

That evening the prince waited outside the palace, and just before sunset, a slender maiden came and sat upon the roof. She wore a sari of shimmering silk, and on her forehead was a golden band set with diamonds and pearls. It seemed as if a silvery radiance shone all around her; in her presence, night became day.

The prince gazed upon Princess Maya. In fact, he could not take his eyes off her, she was so beautiful.

At midnight, long after the princess had gone in, he took the bag and said, "Bag! Give me a shawl of shimmering silk, the very match of Princess Maya's sari!" And there—inside the bag—was a shawl of shimmering silk.

Then he unrolled the carpet, sat down cross-legged, and said, "Carpet! Take me to Princess Maya!"

The carpet rose until it was higher than the rooftops and then flew over the city until it reached the palace. There it sailed through an open window and gently landed on the floor of Princess Maya's room!

Silent as a cat, the prince walked over and placed the shawl beside the sleeping princess. Then he sat back down on the carpet, and off he went.

The next evening the prince again stood outside the palace and gazed upon the beautiful princess; and at midnight he said to the bag, "Bag! Give me a necklace of diamonds and pearls, the very match of Princess Maya's golden headband!" And there it was—a matching golden necklace set with diamonds and pearls.

Again he unrolled his carpet, sat down cross-legged, and commanded, "Carpet! Take me to Princess Maya!" And again off the carpet flew, right into her room. The prince placed the necklace beside the sleeping princess. Then—back on the carpet, and off he went.

On the third evening the prince again stood outside and gazed upon

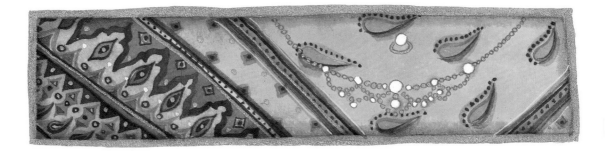

the beautiful princess; at midnight he said, "Bag! Give me a golden ring set with the finest diamonds in the world!" And there it was—a splendid glittering ring.

Again he unrolled his carpet, sat down cross-legged, and flew to the palace and into her room. But this time he did not place the gift beside the sleeping princess. Instead, he lifted her hand and slipped the ring onto one of her fingers.

Princess Maya stirred and opened her eyes. And when she saw the handsome young prince who held her hand, she said, "So, you are the one who gave me the shawl and the necklace, and now this ring. Tell

me, is there something you want, something I can give you in return?"

"There is," said the prince. "You yourself are the gift I seek, for you are the one I wish to marry."

Princess Maya was rather startled by the prince's words, but after they had talked together for much of the night, she agreed to marry this handsome, generous young man. In the morning she took him to her father, the raja of that land, and asked for his consent to their marriage.

But the raja said, "This man is a stranger, one who came like a thief in the night. You may not marry him."

The princess pleaded with her father until at last he declared that if the prince could prove that he was a man of courage and strength, then she could marry him.

The raja said to the prince, "Outside the city there lives a fearsome ogre. He is tall as two, broad as three, and has the strength of six. My people live in fear of him. Day in, day out, he comes and kills and lays waste to their land. If you can capture this ogre, you may marry my daughter."

The prince thought to himself, Capture an ogre? This is a task I can surely do! And, with the stick in his hand, he walked out from the city.

He had not gone far when the mighty ogre saw him and came bounding toward him, roaring and bellowing in a great fury.

"Stick! Do your work!" said the prince. The stick went flying through

the air, and it beat the ogre until he fell helpless to the ground.

The prince said, "Rope! Do your work!" And the rope twirled itself off the stick and, quick as lightning, coiled itself around the ogre until he was bound, head to toe, so tightly that he couldn't even move his little finger.

What then could the raja say? He had to agree to the marriage of the prince and his beautiful daughter, Princess Maya. There was a fine wedding. For four whole weeks, there was feasting and rejoicing throughout the land.

At last the time came when the prince had to take his new bride to his own land. They traveled in a long and magnificent procession, the prince and Princess Maya and their attendants leading the way, riding

the finest black horses ever seen. Behind them trooped a hundred camels, bells jingling, all laden with treasures the raja had heaped upon them.

Now, when, all those weeks ago, the prince's horse had returned to the royal stables without a rider, his mother and father had been certain that their son was dead. So just imagine their happiness when they saw him approaching with his beautiful bride.

The years passed, and the prince and beautiful Princess Maya lived together, happy and content. The prince always kept the bag, the stick, and the carpet ready at hand. And the bag and the carpet were often useful, but—since his was a peaceful country and he had no enemies— he never again needed to use the stick.

Indian

✦ *The Halloween Witches* ✦

One Halloween night, when the moon didn't shine and the wild wind howled, a band of old witches got together in a little cabin down in a hollow behind the dark pines. While a big supper was cooking on the stove, they sat around the fire, telling tall tales and big lies about their friends and neighbors and boasting about the spells they were going to conjure up soon as midnight came along.

By and by, a stranger, one who went about the world doing good, happened to come upon the cabin behind the dark pines. So he knocked at the door.

The witches called out, "Who's there? Who-oo? Who-oo?"

A voice replied, "A stranger. One who is hungry and cold."

Then the witches all laughed and sang out, "We're a-cookin' for ourselves! We'll not cook for you!"

The voice said no more, but the knocking kept on, steady and soft.

The old witches took no notice. They emptied the frying pan, reached for the fresh-baked bread, and began to eat. And, my goodness, how they did eat!

Same time, the knocking kept on, steady and soft, until by and by one of the witches called out, "Who's that a-knockin'? Who-oo? Who-oo?"

Then there came a sort of whistling, wailing sound:

"*Let me in, do-oo!*
I'm cold through and throo-oo-ugh
And I'm hungry too-oo!"

The witches all laughed again and sang out, "Go away, do! We're a-cookin' for ourselves! We'll not cook for you!"

Then they shuffled up closer to the fire and did some more eating. Same time, the knocking kept on, steady and soft, until by and by the witches began to feel uneasy.

One of them said, "Let's give the stranger something and get him to go away before he spoils our spells when midnight comes along."

And she took a little, little, *little* piece of dough, about as big as a pea, and put it in the frying pan and set it on the stove. But soon as she put the dough in the pan, it began to swell. It swelled over the pan. It swelled over the stove. It plumped down on the floor and, swift and strong, swelled and rolled into every corner of the room.

Then the old witches got scared and ran to the door. But the door was tight shut.

They were still scared, so they hitched up their skirts and jumped up on the chair seats and perched there, arms akimbo. And still the dough swelled and rolled, rising up and up until it came over the seats of the chairs.

So then the witches climbed on the backs of the chairs and scrunched

up small as they could while their eyes got bigger and rounder with scaredness. And still the dough swelled and rolled. Same time, the knocking kept on, steady and soft.

The witches called out again, "Who's that a-knockin'? Who-oo? Who-oo?"

Then the knocking stopped, and the witches heard these words creeping through every crack and cranny of the house:

"You refuse to give, you refuse to lend;
Criticize your neighbor, criticize your friend.
Now hush your tattling, hush your talk;
You'll never more have strength to walk!"

There and then, the witches' legs began to shrink, until they were so small and weak, they could scarcely hop. They looked at each other and were so surprised at what they saw, they blinked their eyes and turned their heads right around, front to back. For you see, they were no longer witches. They all had turned into owls.

Then the owls heard these words creeping through the house:

"Because you wouldn't open your door,
You shan't live in a house no more.
So fly out any window you see,
And live your life in a hollow tree!"

Well, by this time, the dough had risen so high that there was only a little gap left at the top of an open window. So the owls spread their wings and flew toward it, pushing and jostling, each one scared she wouldn't get out. But, one after the other, they somehow managed to twist out of that window and fly off into the woods, still calling out, "Who's that a-knockin'? Who-oo? Who-oo?"

And even to this day, in the dark of night, those owls still swoop and fly, calling, always calling, "Who-oo? Who-oo?"

Except at Halloween. On that one night, those owls turn back into witches and sneak through the woods, weaving and conjuring up all their wicked and most mischievous spells.

African-American

✦ *Koala* ✦

Koala was a boy who lived long ago, in the dreamtime. He had no mother or father. He had no brothers or sisters. He was alone in the tribe. And because of this, he did exactly what he wanted and didn't listen to anyone. He was always up to mischief of one kind or another.

Now, one year, when the dry time came, all the streams and rivers and billabongs dried up, and the people had to walk a long way to the water holes in order to get enough to drink. Everyone who was big and strong enough went and brought some water back—everyone except for Koala. He didn't like to go walking. He stayed behind in the camp, making mischief. And when the others came back, he went around begging for a drink until someone took pity and gave him one.

But a day came when no one would give Koala water. Everyone said he should pick up his own coolamon and go and get his own water.

The next morning, the men went hunting and the women and children went off to dig for roots. There was only one person left in the camp —Koala. And by this time he was feeling very thirsty, so he went around the camp, looking for water. But he couldn't find any. All the precious water had been very carefully hidden.

He looked here, there, everywhere. He didn't give up. And in the end he found a whole lot of coolamons full of water, hidden in the bush under some shady trees.

So Koala had a good, long drink. And when he couldn't drink another drop, he said, "I know what I'll do. I'll hide the water in my own secret place. Then I won't be thirsty again for a long time."

He took a full coolamon, climbed up a small gum tree, and hid the coolamon on a branch among the leaves. Then he took the rest of the full coolamons, one after the other, and hid them in the tree.

He had just hidden the last one when the tree stirred itself, and— strong magic—it sprang up and up and up, until it became an enormous tree, as wide and tall as many small trees put together. Koala hung on tight, and when the tree stopped growing, he found himself near the top, with the coolamons around him. He thought he could climb down. But could he climb up again? He wasn't sure about that. So he sat down on a big branch, right up against the trunk, and had a little snooze.

At sunset, when everyone returned to the camp, they were so hot and thirsty, they went straight to the hiding place to get a drink. But they found only a few empty coolamons there.

Everyone immediately had the same thought. "Koala! Where is Koala?"

And they looked around and saw an enormous tree where there had only been a small tree before, and near the top sat Koala and all the coolamons!

"Koala!" they shouted. "Bring down our water!"

But Koala laughed. He felt safe at the top of that enormous tree. "If you want the water," he called out, "come and get it yourselves!"

Then a young man said, "I'll bring down the water. It is a very tall tree, but I can climb it!"

And his friend said, "And I'll bring down that rascal Koala, so that we can deal with him!"

Together they climbed the tree while Koala peered down through the branches, watching them. When they had almost reached the top, Koala lifted a coolamon and poured water down the trunk and over the two young men. Their hands slipped on the smooth, wet bark. They lost their grip and went sliding down to the bottom of the tree.

Then two brothers offered to climb. But they didn't go straight up, hand over hand. They were cunning and swung themselves around and around the trunk, in a spiral. Koala waited until they had almost reached him, and then he poured water over them. But they swung themselves around the trunk so swiftly that the water missed them. They climbed on and up, coming closer and closer. Koala was afraid, and he began to moan and wail and cry.

The next thing, one of the brothers reached out and grabbed him. Koala struggled hard and managed to break free. But then he lost his balance and fell, bouncing from branch to branch, right to the ground.

Every single bone in his body hurt. But Koala didn't wait. He jumped up and ran. Everyone was so angry, they chased after him, shaking their fists and shouting. They were determined to catch Koala. And they almost did. But just in time he reached another tree and scurried up it, fast as he could.

And then, before their eyes—strong magic again!—Koala was changing. Rough gray hair covered his body. His ears stood up, all fringed and furry, above two round black eyes and a shiny small black nose. He was no longer Koala the boy. He had become Koala the bear.

Even today, he is Koala the bear. And—would you believe it?—he still won't go looking for water if he can help it. Whenever he is thirsty, he just nibbles some juicy leaves from a gum tree, and that's usually enough for him.

But he has never forgotten the day when he was in trouble and was nearly caught. If anyone begins to climb his tree, he makes a great fuss and moans and wails and cries, just as he did when he was a little boy called Koala.

Australian

✦ *Baba Yaga Bony-Legs* ✦

Once upon a time and far, far away, at the edge of a dark forest, there lived a girl called Masha and her father and stepmother. And that stepmother! Well, when Father was there, she smiled and spoke sweet as honey. But when Father was away, it was "Do this, Masha! Do that!" And whatever Masha did, it was never good enough. Sharp words were all Stepmother had for Masha.

One day when Father had gone to visit friends in a distant village, Stepmother said, "Tomorrow, Masha, I shall make you a new dress. But first, you must borrow a needle and some thread from my sister, who lives in the forest."

"Borrow a needle and thread!" cried Masha. She was surprised. "There are plenty of needles and a whole lot of thread in the cupboard," she said.

"Don't argue!" snapped Stepmother. "Just go! And remember to tell my sister I sent you!"

"But how shall I know the way?" asked Masha.

"That's easy," said Stepmother. "Take the path at the back of the house and follow your nose."

Now, Masha was not stupid. She knew her stepmother was trying to get rid of her. Who lived in the forest? Only the wolf . . . and the

bear . . . *and* Baba Yaga Bony-Legs, the old witch. But what could Masha do? She knew she had to go.

So she combed her golden hair, plaited it in a long, thick braid, and tied it with a bright red ribbon. Then she asked her stepmother to give her some food for the journey. And what was she given? A lump of stale bread and a bone with only a tiny scrap of meat left on it. That was all. But Masha took the food and wrapped it in an old cotton kerchief that had belonged to her own mother. And then she set off.

She took the path at the back of the house and followed it straight ahead through the forest. She walked and walked, one foot in front of the other, until she was so tired that she had to sit down and rest.

While she was sitting there, a gray mouse crept out from under a bush and sniffed the air.

"You look hungry," said Masha, and, opening her kerchief, she broke off some bread crumbs and scattered them on the ground.

When the mouse had eaten the crumbs, he looked up and spoke. "Girl with the golden hair, why are you walking alone through the dark forest?"

"My stepmother has sent me to borrow a needle and thread from her sister, who lives in the forest," explained Masha.

"Ahhh," sighed the mouse. "She is sending you to Baba Yaga Bony-Legs. But you are a girl with a kind heart, so don't be afraid." And with a whisk of his tail, he was gone.

Masha wrapped the bone and the rest of the bread in her kerchief and walked on.

After a while, she came to a stand of birch trees. Beyond that, she came to a clearing in the forest. In the middle of the clearing, there was a hut with staring windows, perched on top of two great chicken legs. The hut was turning around and around, around and around.

Masha drew herself up and said, "Little house, stand with back to forest and face to me!" She wanted to make the hut stop turning.

And the hut stood still.

Now, there was a high gate and a fence of sharp-pointed stakes around the clearing, and when Masha opened the gate, it gave a loud *c-r-e-a-k!*

"Gate," she said, as she closed it behind her, "you need some oil on your hinges!"

Masha walked toward the hut, and a skinny-looking dog came bounding up to her, barking furiously.

"You look hungry," said Masha, and, opening her kerchief, she took out the bone and gave it to him.

The dog stopped barking, picked up the bone, and set to work on it.

Masha walked on. She stepped into the hut that was perched on chicken legs, and there was Baba Yaga, the old witch herself. She was weaving on a loom that went *clickety-clack! clickety-clack!* She was *huge*, with long bony legs and a mouth full of iron teeth.

"Who are you?" snarled Baba Yaga. "And who sent you?"

"My name is Masha," answered the girl. "And my stepmother, your sister, sent me to borrow a needle and thread."

"To borrow a needle and thread. *Hmmm* . . . I know what that means! Now, while I get ready, you must work. Just do the weaving, while I go to the bathhouse and take a bath. And then it will be time for me to have my supper!" And off she went.

Masha began to weave, *clickety-clack! clickety-clack!* And after a while, a thin black cat came strolling into the house.

"You look hungry," said Masha, and she reached for her kerchief, took out the stale bread, and gave it to the cat.

The cat ate every last bit, and when he had finished, he looked up and said, "This is not a good place to be. You must run away before Baba Yaga returns and eats you with her iron teeth."

"But if I run away, surely she will chase me and catch me," said Masha.

"On the table there is a comb and an embroidered towel," said the cat. "Take them, and if Baba Yaga catches up with you in the forest, first throw down the towel and then throw down the comb."

"But what about the weaving? As soon as the clickety-clacking stops, she will be out of the bathhouse and after me before I can reach the gate."

The cat thought for a moment. "I shall do the weaving," he said.

"Thank you, good cat," said Masha, taking the towel and the comb. "Now, there is one more thing I must do before I leave." And she picked up a bottle of oil that was standing beside Baba Yaga's lamp.

Meanwhile, the cat began to work at the loom. But he had no idea how to weave, and in no time at all he had got the threads twisted and tangled. What a mess and muddle he made of it! But he still kept the loom going *clickety-clack! clickety-clack!*

When Masha stepped out of Baba Yaga's hut, the skinny-looking dog came bounding up to her. He wagged his tail and licked her hand. At the gate, she poured the oil on its hinges, and when she opened the gate, it didn't creak. But when she came to the stand of birch trees, they stretched out their branches and caught hold of her and would not let

her pass. So Masha undid the ribbon at the bottom of her golden plait and tied a big floppy bow around one of the branches. And then the birch trees lifted their branches, rustled their leaves, and let her pass.

Then Masha ran—and ran—and ran.

When Baba Yaga came out of the bathhouse, she heard the loom clacking, so she didn't hurry. "Are you weaving, my little dear?" she called through the window.

"Yes, Auntie," answered the cat, trying to talk like Masha. But his voice came out sort of squeaky, and Baba Yaga knew it was her own cat.

She strode into the house, picked up a ladle, and flung it at him. "Why did you let Masha leave?" she snarled. "Why didn't you scratch her eyes out?"

The cat curled up his tail, arched his back, and said, "For years and years I have served you, and you've never given me even a burned crust. But Masha gave me her own bread."

On went Baba Yaga. *Stamp! Stamp!*

"Dog, why did you let Masha leave?" she snarled. "Why didn't you bark and bite her?"

The dog looked Baba Yaga straight in the eye and said, "For years and years I have served you, and you've never given me even a dry old bone.

But Masha gave me a fresh bone with meat on it."

On went Baba Yaga. *Stamp! Stamp!*

"Gate, why did you let Masha leave?" she snarled. "Why didn't you creak?"

The gate said, "For years and years I have served you, and you have done nothing for me. But Masha bathed my hinges with oil."

Baba Yaga flung open the gate and went through. *Stamp! Stamp!*

"Birch trees, why did you let Masha leave?" she snarled. "Why didn't you entrap her with your branches?"

The birch trees said, "For years and years we have served you, Baba

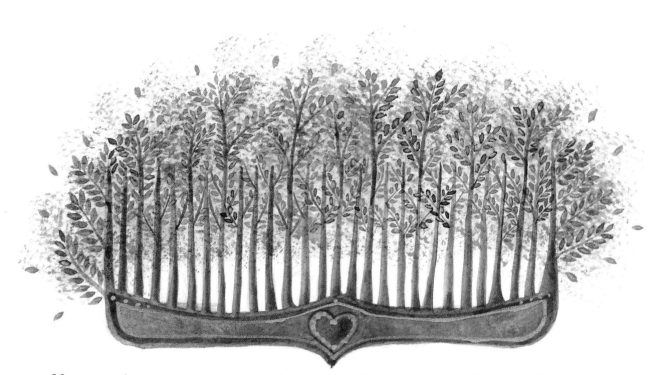

Yaga, and you never even tied a piece of string on us. But Masha took
her own bright ribbon and tied it on one of our branches."

Then Baba Yaga jumped into her stone mortar, picked up the pestle,
and, using it to drive herself forward, off she went through the forest . . . *whoo-oosh!*

As soon as Masha heard the noise, she looked back. When she saw
Baba Yaga on the path behind her, she threw down the towel. Suddenly
a great wide river flowed there, brimful of water.

Baba Yaga's mortar was too heavy to float across, so she had to think
of something else. She found her cattle and drove them to the river,
where they drank and drank until the water was gone. Then she was on
her way once more . . . *whoo-oosh!*

Again Masha heard the noise and looked back. When she saw Baba
Yaga coming, she threw down the comb. And suddenly there sprang up
a great host of tall trees, hundreds and thousands of them, so close
together it would have been hard for even a fly to pass through.

Baba Yaga sharpened her iron teeth. She bit into a tree and hurled it

aside. She sharpened her teeth again, bit into another tree, and hurled it aside. On and on she went, sharpening, biting, and hurling. But the trees were so many and so close that she still could not get through. In the end, shouting and snarling, she turned around and went home.

And Masha? Well, she ran—and ran—and ran.

It was almost dark by the time she reached the edge of the forest. The lamps were lit in her own house, and her father was outside, looking all around.

As soon as he saw her, he called out, "Where have you been? What happened? I have been looking for you everywhere."

Masha answered, "Stepmother sent me to her own sister in the forest to borrow a needle and thread, and that sister was Baba Yaga Bony-Legs, the witch. It was hard to escape, but with the help of some friends, I managed at last."

When her father heard this, he was very angry. He strode into the house—but Stepmother was already gone.

She had seen Masha and had heard her talking to Father. She knew she had been found out and straightaway had run off into the forest. And whether she reached the house of her own sister, Baba Yaga Bony-Legs, or whether the wolf or the bear got her first, no one ever knew.

Masha and her father never saw her again. From that time on, they lived together in peace and contentment in their house at the edge of the dark forest.

Russian

✦ *The Yellow Thunder Dragon* ✦

Once, long ago, there was a quiet, thoughtful boy called Chang. Chang was always daydreaming, always wishing that something surprising and extraordinary would happen to him. But nothing ever did . . . until one day when he was thirteen years old.

Chang lived with his grandmother and his father, Yin, who was a farmer. Grandmother was old and wise, and because Chang's mother had died, she had always taken care of him and given him extra love.

Well, one hot afternoon, when Grandmother was asleep and his father was busy in the house, Chang wandered out to the garden. He gazed across the plains and winding river to the mountains beyond. He was just standing at the garden gate, quietly daydreaming, when a handsome young man dressed all in yellow came up the road on horseback. Four servants walked beside him, one of them holding a splendid yellow umbrella over his head to shield him from the sun.

There was something strange about these travelers. Chang studied them carefully. At first sight the horse looked white, but as it moved, a haze of color shimmered and shone around it, like sunshine on water. Its hooves didn't seem to touch the ground. And the servants' feet seemed not to touch the ground either. It was as if they all walked on air.

The travelers stopped at the gate, and the young man said, "I am weary, Chang, son of Yin. May I enter your father's garden and rest?"

Chang was surprised the young man knew his name, but he bowed and opened the gate, saying, "Enter, my lord."

The young man swung down lightly from his horse, whereupon a servant tethered it to the gatepost. Then they all seated themselves in the courtyard, next to the house.

As soon as Chang's father heard voices, he came out and welcomed the visitors. He sent Chang to bring refreshments, and then he sat down to talk to the handsome young man.

Now, while the others ate and drank, Chang stood a little way off, hands tucked in his sleeves, and watched. Here at last were many surprising and extraordinary things. The young man's clothes were woven all in one piece, without any seams. And his feet had not touched the

ground when he walked. As for the horse, its body was not covered with hair but with shiny white scales, each with five tiny spots of color.

When the travelers had finished their refreshments, the young man dressed all in yellow thanked Yin for his hospitality. Then the whole party rose and took their leave. The servant carrying the splendid yellow umbrella turned it upside down before crossing the gate, and when he reached the road, he turned it right side up again.

The handsome young man mounted his horse. "I shall come again tomorrow," he said, looking at Chang.

Chang bowed. "Come, my lord," he answered. And he stood and watched as the young man and his servants continued up the road toward the mountains. Up and up they went—and then, suddenly, they rose into the air and vanished among the gathering rain clouds.

When Chang went back into the house, his father said to him, "Those were strange visitors. Though I've never seen that young man before, he knew my name and everything about me. You were watching them. Tell me, did you notice anything unusual?"

"Yes, Father. The men's feet and the horse's hooves never touched the ground, and besides—"

"Their feet didn't touch the ground!" exclaimed Yin. "Then they were not men. They were spirits! We must tell your grandmother. She knows about such things."

Grandmother was in a deep sleep and didn't want to be wakened. But at last she stirred and yawned.

"Grandmother," said Chang. "Today we were visited by strangers whose feet did not touch the ground."

At that, Grandmother was wide-awake. "Tell me more," she urged.

So Chang told her about the handsome young man and the seamless yellow clothes; the splendid umbrella; the four servants and the white horse; and how they all rose into the air and vanished among the rain clouds.

"Seamless clothes are magic clothes," said Grandmother. "And yellow is a sacred color. The young man must be the Yellow Thunder Dragon. His horse is a dragon horse, and his servants are the four winds. A great storm will come. . . ." She frowned. "Have you told me everything?"

"There is something else," said Chang. "The servant who was carrying the umbrella turned it upside down before leaving our garden."

"Ah, that is a good omen," said Grandmother. And with that, she closed her eyes and fell back to sleep.

In the evening, when Chang's father looked out and saw dark clouds above the western mountains, he decided that he and his son should stay up and wait for the storm. In honor of the Yellow Thunder Dragon, Chang put on a yellow robe that his grandmother had made him. Then he lit a yellow lantern and burned incense and read magic charms from an ancient yellow book.

Meanwhile, Grandmother slept.

Later that night the storm finally broke. Chang closed his book and looked out the window with his father. Lightning flamed. Thunder rolled and crashed and boomed. And then the rain came. Swollen streams

gushed down the mountainsides. The river rose higher and higher, until it finally burst its banks and flooded the fields, sweeping away everything in its path: trees, houses, and all living creatures.

Time passed. The thunder quieted and the lightning moved on. But still the rain fell. When daylight came, Yin and Chang looked out the door. They could see that the floodwater reached right up to their garden.

"We should have fled to the mountains last night," said Yin. "We would have been safe there. But now it is too late. What shall we do?"

Chang stepped into the garden and looked up at the sky. Above their house he saw a yellow dragon, its hood spread out as if to protect

them. For one brief moment he saw the dragon—then it was gone.

"Father!" he cried. "I have seen the dragon!"

"You are tired and dreaming, my son," said Yin.

"But look! It is not raining on our house!" exclaimed Chang.

His father came out into the garden and saw for himself. Although it was raining everywhere else, no rain fell on their roof.

"So the dragon is guarding us," Yin said. "It was good that you welcomed him and his servants yesterday, my son."

At midday the rain stopped. Only then did Yin and his son realize that in all the plain their house alone remained undamaged. It was as if the storm had never been. The floodwater had come up to their garden and then swept around it, as though held back by a strong invisible wall.

Later that afternoon the sun came out. Chang went and stood once again by the garden gate. He looked to the west and saw the young man dressed all in yellow ride down from the mountains, his four servants beside him. As before, their feet did not touch the ground. They reached the gate and stopped.

"I told you that I would come again," said the young man. "But this time I shall not enter your garden."

Chang bowed. "As it pleases you," he said.

The young man took a scale from his horse's neck and gave it to Chang. "Keep this safely," he said, "and use it wisely."

Chang bowed again.

The young man and his servants continued on their way, crossing the floodwater, the horse's hooves and the servants' feet seeming to walk on air. When they came to a place where there was a deep, still pool, they sank down into the water and vanished.

Chang hurried inside and found a small wooden box lined with silk. Carefully he laid the scale in the box. Then he went to his father and told him that the Yellow Thunder Dragon had returned to his pool.

"We must tell Grandmother," said Yin.

Grandmother was still asleep. But when at last she stirred and opened her eyes, Chang told her everything that had happened and showed her the small shiny scale.

"Now when the emperor sends for you both," said Grandmother, "all will be well."

"And why should the emperor send for us?" asked Yin.

"You shall see," answered Grandmother. Whereupon she closed her eyes and fell asleep once again.

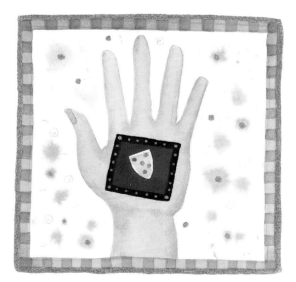

News travels fast. It was not long before the emperor heard about the storm and the great flood it had caused.

The emperor also heard about a strange marvel that had been seen by the people who had fled up the mountains to escape the storm. It seemed that rain had fallen everywhere but on one house—the house of Yin, the farmer. Besides this, the floodwater had swept right around his house and garden, as if deflected by a strong invisible wall.

The emperor thought there must be some powerful magic at work in this, so he sent messengers with orders to bring Yin and all who lived in his house back to the imperial palace.

Well, Grandmother refused to go. She wanted to sleep. But Chang and his father set off straightaway.

It was early evening when they reached the palace. But the emperor received them immediately. He asked Yin to tell him what had happened during the storm.

"My lord," said Yin, "the story belongs to my son, Chang. He is the one who must tell it."

So Chang told the story of the Yellow Thunder Dragon, starting at the beginning. By the time he got to the end, darkness had fallen. Then he took the small shiny scale out of the box, and it shone so brightly that it lit the throne room like the noonday sun.

"Chang, son of Yin," said the emperor, "you shall remain here and become one of my royal magicians, for the Yellow Thunder Dragon has given you a scale that holds within it powerful magic."

And so Chang, though only thirteen, became a royal magician.

As time passed, he found that there was indeed powerful magic in the scale from the dragon horse. When he held it in his hand, he could do many things. He could heal the sick. He could foretell the future. He could even win mighty victories for the emperor's army.

The emperor rewarded Chang generously and gave him a great house near the imperial palace. His father and grandmother lived with him there..Yin lived the comfortable life of a rich lord. And Grandmother? Well, most of the time she slept. But when she did wake, she shared with Chang the wisdom and knowledge of her many years.

Chinese

Something about the Stories and Where They Came From

THE LEMON PRINCESS

It is not always possible to say exactly where a story originated. This popular story has been collected in many countries, from Spain to Turkey and Iran. The Arab domination of much of Spain and Portugal, which lasted about seven hundred years, probably brought the story into that area, and from there it doubtless spread throughout southern Europe. The killing of the heroine by a servant girl is a common motif in Arab stories, and the importance of water would seem to indicate an area close to deserts. The magic fruit varies. It can be oranges, or even pumpkins. I chose a version from *Fairy Tales from Turkey*, translated by Margery Kent (1946), that uses a lemon as the magic fruit.

FEATHER WOMAN AND THE MORNING STAR

The story of the star husband was particularly widespread among North American Indians living in the Great Plains area. Sometimes the girl reached the sky by climbing into a tree that simply stretched upward. The moon was regarded by many Indian tribes as a patron of women and of crops. This version is retold from Walter McClintock's *The Old North Trail; or, Life, Legends and Religion of the Blackfeet Indians* (1910).

THE KINGDOM UNDER THE SEA

This is a favorite story in Japan. The retelling is based mainly on F. H. Davis's *Myths and Legends of Japan* (1917). Urashima's lacquered box usually contains only mist or smoke, and he immediately grows old and dies. I have borrowed the lovely ending where he finally becomes a crane from a version, briefly referred to, in Keigo Seki's *Folktales of Japan*, translated by Robert J. Adams (1963).

UNANANA AND THE ENORMOUS ONE-TUSKED ELEPHANT

Many African tales, including this one, were written down for the first time by white missionaries or administrators. This retelling is based on the tale found in Henry Callaway's *Nursery Tales, Traditions and Histories of the Zulus in Their Own Words* (1868). Elephants make well-defined roads through the bush, and the male when angry is dangerous.

KATE CRACKERNUTS

It is unusual in fairy tales for stepsisters to be fond of each other, and it is also unusual for them to share the same first name. This version is based on two tales, both from regions of Scotland: one from the Orkney Islands (in *Folklore*, September 1890) and the other from Angus (in *Longman's Magazine*, November 1888 to April 1889). Resourceful, determined girls are found more frequently in Scottish fairy tales than in those from other countries.

THE KING WHO WANTED TO TOUCH THE MOON

This story from the Dominican Republic, based on the version in Manuel de Andrade's *Folklore of the Dominican Republic* (1930), traveled from West Africa. In one version collected in what is now Zaire, the king has a bamboo tower built in order to reach the treasure that is sparkling in the sky.

THREE GOLDEN APPLES

The magic fruit can be peaches, oranges, apples, or figs, while the other brothers' baskets may contain cowpats or horse dung! French fairy tales are particularly lively, inventive, and humorous. Dozens of different versions of this story have been collected in France. A typical version is in *Revue des Traditions Populaires* (1891).

THE MAGIC FRUIT

This story was first recorded by Francisco de Avila, in 1608 (see H. B. Alexander's *Mythology of All Races*, volume 11, 1920). Cavillaca and Coniraya were *huacas* who lived in the world as humans. Although I have called them great magicians, huacas were more like spirits or gods. The fruit described in this version is that of the lucuma, noted for its sweetness.

SEVEN CLEVER BROTHERS

While there are numerous stories, particularly in northern Europe, of traveling companions with amazing skills, this one—with its central emphasis on the importance of seven brothers staying good friends—is unusual. The source is G. Friedlander's *Jewish Fairy Tales and Stories* (1918).

THE PRINCE AND THE FLYING CARPET

Stealing magic objects by cheating the quarrelsome owners is a motif that occurs widely in fairy tales. Instead of a carpet, bag, and stick, there may be a traveling cap, a self-filling purse, and a horn or whistle that, when blown, will summon soldiers. This version is from Maive S. H. Stokes's *Indian Fairy Tales* (1879).

THE HALLOWEEN WITCHES

Here a European tale (in an English version, a baker's miserly daughter becomes an owl) meets the African "conjure wife" tale to create a new story typical of the African-American folktale. This retelling is based on two versions: one in Martha Young's *Plantation Bird Legends* (1916) and the other in Francis G. Wickes's *Holiday Stories* (1921).

KOALA

Central to this story is the importance of being careful with water in the dry season. It comes from R. Brough Smyth's *The Aborigines of Victoria* (1878).

BABA YAGA BONY-LEGS

No other country has a witch quite like the Russian Baba Yaga. In one story, the fence around her house is made of human bones, and on the spikes are human skulls with staring eyes! This is retold mainly from W. R. Ralston's *Russian Folk Tales* (1873).

THE YELLOW THUNDER DRAGON

Chinese dragons are quite different from the European fire-breathing variety. They are associated with water, sleeping in deep pools, and emerging to bring rain. They are godlike creatures and can adopt a human form. This version is from Donald A. Mackenzie's *Myths of China and Japan* (1923).